Unsuitable Friends

Linda

— with kindest
thoughts

Fiona Kidman.

Also by Fiona Kidman

Search for Sister Blue (play)
Honey and Bitters (poems)
On the Tightrope (poems)
A Breed of Women (novel)
Mandarin Summer (novel)
Mrs Dixon & Friend (short stories)
Paddy's Puzzle (novel)
Gone North (non-fiction)
Going to the Chathams (poems)
The Book of Secrets (novel)

CONTENTS

At the Lake So Blue 9

A Moving Life 21

There He Comes 32

The Whiteness 42

At the Homestead Hotel 50

Beyond the Wall 59

The Courting of Nora 74

The Prize Ring 88

Puff Adder 100

Hats 111

Needles and Glass 116

Body Searches 125

Earthly Shadows 135

The Tennis Player 145

The Sugar Club 156

Pudding 158

Acknowledgement is made to the publications in which some of these stories first appeared. 'At the Homestead Hotel', 'Needles and Glass', 'Hats', *NZ Listener*; 'The Courting of Nora', *North & South*; 'The Whiteness', *Landfall*; 'Pudding', *Antipodes New Writing 1*; 'Puff Adder', *New Women's Fiction* (New Women's Press); 'Earthly Shadows', *New Zealand Outlook*; 'A Moving Life', *More*.

Acknowledgement is also made to the following for permission to reproduce copyright material: 'Pretend', J. Albert & Son Pty. Ltd; 'Twilight Time', Castle Music Pty. Ltd.

'Earthly Shadows' was winner of the 1987 Mobil/*New Zealand Outlook* Short Story Award.

Thanks are especially due to Nicky Ling, who was the driving force and inspiration behind 'Hats'.

While these stories were being written the author was the recipient of a grant from the New Zealand Literary Fund.

For Giles and Vannessa & Zach and Toby

At the Lake So Blue

When I was asked if I would go in the bathing beauty contest I said I would think about it. To tell the truth I was flattered. It also seemed to be exactly the kind of thing my parents would disapprove of me doing.

How it happened was like this. I had been going around with two girls called Linda and Sugar (Sugar's real name was Janet) all summer. This was the end of 1958, turning 1959. Linda was a stocky blonde with a pert face. She was engaged but her fiancé was working in the South Island, because there was big money in the meatworks down there at the time, and he was saving to buy them a house; he wanted her to have everything in it right from the start. It was as if she was married, but not quite. Sugar was her old schoolfriend and was going to be her bridesmaid. I thought she was the prettiest girl I knew.

I had other friends but they were doing different things at the time. Some had just got married and others were away on overseas travel. I was a librarian and I wasn't meant to be thinking about either of these activities because I had promised my father I would pass my library exams. I never meant to make a promise like that but I hadn't kept my first two jobs and I supposed I should try hard at something. I was better at being a librarian than I expected, and before I knew where I was two years had slid past and my qualifications began to mount up. It would be a shame to throw the course away before you were finished, my father said. When you've gone so far.

It was considered a brainy sort of job, and I thought of myself as having a brainy face, which was not a great comfort when I was with Linda and Sugar.

They were great dancers though, and Linda had won a rock-'n'roll jamboree once with her fiancé before he went south. Sugar was a brilliant water-skier. She said the club was looking for new members and she could get me in if I liked.

You see, this was the other side of me to the librarian who was cultivating a slightly starchy manner behind my glasses. I loved to dance, and to swim. Rhythm at night, and the water by day. It was my idea of heaven. I believed, honestly believed, that if you went out after the best of all possible worlds, you could get everything you wanted.

Linda's fiancé had said she wasn't to give up dancing just because he wasn't around, so long as she stayed with 'the girls'. This was where Sugar came into it. She acted as a chaperone. And that was where I came into it, because Sugar said, it was all very well for her to go around with Linda but it cramped her style a bit always being with an engaged girl. Sugar said she wanted to have fun forever.

We teamed up with three boys who were on holiday. They were called Smitty and Miles and Bozo. Smitty was a basketballer and he was off on a scholarship to the States in the New Year, and Miles and Bozo were both engaged to girls in the town from which they came. They were having a last good time together before they all got on with the serious business of life, although it was clear that the other two were worried about Smitty, as well as proud of him. It was hardly a job he was going into, they said, it takes some chaps longer to get things out of their systems than others.

When they suggested we go around with them it was agreed that it was an ideal arrangement for everybody, nobody wanted commitments and, really, it was just laughs we were having; laughs for a summer. We were having fun.

Nobody actually asked me what I thought about it but I trusted Linda and Sugar's judgment. It bothered me a little that I spent most of my time with Bozo but in return for the good times it seemed churlish to complain. Besides, he owned the car in which we all travelled. This was considered a bonus for me, because I got to sit in the front. And I never got left behind.

Miles and Smitty were very cool, and Smitty, as befitted a basketballer, was immensely tall. People noticed Sugar and Smitty and Linda and Miles, in couples, as they strolled through the carnival that ran all summer in town, whereas Bozo and I got lost in the crowd.

No matter. We danced. We swam. We went to the Blue Lake. The Blue Lake is one of two beautiful lakes that lie in a basin beside each other close to the town. The other is the Green Lake. The Green Lake is, as its name suggests, coloured like an emerald, and like the jewel, which is said to be unlucky, so is the water of that lake not to be touched for fear of retribution. It is a sacred lake.

But the Blue Lake, only a narrow isthmus of land away, shines with perpetual blueness. The ski lanes are crowded, the beaches are clotted with children and their parents. Station wagons sit side by side as far as the eye can see. There is a smell of barbecues and suntan lotion in the air. So it is now, so it was then.

I swam, though I had trouble learning to water-ski. I was what they called a duck's arse skier because although I could hang onto the tows all right I could never stand up. Nobody seemed to worry much, although they laughed. I got an even suntan while the rest of them streaked over the lake behind the boats with the water creaming up around them.

What did I think about? I don't remember. Summer days / summer daze.

I always hesitate when it comes to describing my mother. She is alive still, a spry, if arthritic woman, who has lived half the time in the suburb where I live now, but knows twice as many people as I do. I think she was shy in her way, of the brawny young men who occasionally wandered through the house. I say occasionally, because she and my father were more formal with my friends than their parents were with me, and I didn't always ask them home.

They offered cups of tea, and conversation. My father also believed that entertainment should be provided. Some of the things he came out with made me think I would die of embarrassment.

On Saturday afternoon, in the last week of the year, the sky turned grey and drizzly at the lake, and a small chill wind played round our wet legs. We tried to resist the change in the weather. Linda sat and squashed pimples on Miles' back, and Smitty and Sugar threw stones in the water. But it was useless; we weren't having fun. Someone suggested that we all go to my house which was the nearest to the lake.

My father was a patriotic man. The war was like yesterday to him. He admired valour. When he talked of brave deeds he got a strange high catch in his voice as if it would break with sorrow at any moment. I wished he wouldn't be like that; now I hear my own voice at times, just the same, though from different causes. It is to do with being swept with emotion.

He was, he said when we arrived that afternoon, about to play some records. I introduced him to my unsuitable friends. He cast an eye over them and decided to make the best of things. He played all of *My Fair Lady*. Linda and Miles went outside and smoked, even though it was raining quite hard by then.

My father sang a few snatches of the 'Ascot Gavotte'.

When the record was finished, I called out brightly, 'Rain stopped out there?'

'It's still going, can't you hear it, duffer,' my father said. 'Now listen to this.' And his eyes were shining and his voice caught, and I remember this with love, though I hated him for it then.

He played both sides of the dramatisation of Paul Gallico's novel *The Snow Goose* while I looked at my feet, and stole glances at the others; they were pulling faces at each other. At the end of side one Miles said politely, 'D'you mind if I use the phone, sir?'

I knew he was organising an alibi for them to get away.

'No phone,' said my father triumphantly.

'There's a wait with the Post Office,' I said in quiet desperation. We had been living there for four years.

'Who says?' roared my father. 'I don't believe in 'em.'

'It's not actually raining any more,' said Smitty, and everyone stood up at once.

'D'you have to go?' said my father. 'We've had such a nice time.'

As we rounded the hill above the lake in Bozo's pink and silver Chevvy, the sun shone, suddenly and mysteriously bright again. Nobody was saying much to me, and I knew that it was because they did not know what to say. I guessed they were wishing I had stayed at home.

A few hardy individuals had stayed at the lake until the rain cleared. They sat in the sun, steaming as they dried out. Sugar's friend Frank, who owned the boat used for towing the others when they were skiing, was still there. We sat around him, lighting up. Linda and Sugar and I slid our tops and shorts from over our bathing suits so we could lie in the sun while the action was decided. Our skins shone with a gloss like brown velvet. Sugar and Linda were stretching out close to each other, a little way away from me. I couldn't find it in myself to blame them.

'So who is going to be Miss Blue Lake?' Frank was saying. New Year was approaching and after that would come the

Queen Carnival, which raised money for worthy projects in the town each year. All sorts of groups put up a beauty candidate to contest the crown. Miss Blue Lake often won. There was an aura about Miss Blue Lake.

'Why not you, Linda?' I said, aware that I was currying favour.

'I'm engaged,' she said in a prim voice. But I could see she was not displeased.

'Sugar?'

'I've done that. It was boring.'

'Why not you?' asked Frank, and he turned to me.

I thought he was sending me up. But he wasn't.

The others turned too and I could see them considering the matter.

'Great fig-uah,' said Miles.

'I'm too short,' I said.

'Heels. Put you in stilettos,' said Frank, his enthusiasm mounting.

I saw Sugar and Linda glance at each other. They could see which way things were going.

'What *are* your measurements?' Linda asked.

'Thirty-four, twenty-two, thirty-four.'

Bozo whistled.

But Linda said, 'I could lend you my padded suit.'

Frank shook his head. 'Judges don't like padding. They can always tell.'

'The heels'll push her forward a bit more,' Sugar said. 'We can teach you to walk. It's easy.' She got to her feet and did a cat-walk along the beach. Smitty rolled his eyes and yelled, 'Whee-who-ah, steady there, girl,' and everyone applauded.

'Well that's settled,' said Frank.

'I'm not a blonde,' I said.

Frank's stomach had an unfortunate way of rolling over the top of his swim shorts. He tucked it into place. 'Neither was Sugar,' he said.

There was a brief prickly silence. Sugar said she was Spanish; I'd heard she was a closet Maori. That's what my father said.

Sugar smiled then, as if there was nothing wrong. 'What would your parents say?' she said, addressing me.

Bozo giggled.

It was Smitty who spoke to me kindly. 'D'you want to do it?' he asked. 'Is that what you want?'

Later that night we went dancing. We started at the Ritz Ballroom. The Ritz had a vast glossy floor: the hall doubled for the A & P machinery show in winter. The band sat above the floor on a stage. The Master of Ceremonies (we called him the Emcee) announced the dances: Gentlemen, take your partners for a foxtrot. A valeta. The supper waltz (keep the supper waltz for me; it meant you got to sit with a boy for the interval). Ballin' the Jack. A maxina. All the way through to the last waltz (keep the last dance for me).

The Ritz. It was the place where nice girls told their mothers they were going, and did. Or the place not so nice girls told their mothers they were going to, and left and went down to Tama.

After two foxtrots, I said to the others, 'Let's go to Tama. Shall we? Why don't we go down to Tama?'

I saw Sugar and Linda glance at each other, uncertain. I thought, you bitches. I knew they went to Tama. But they didn't know for sure what Miles and Smitty and Bozo would think.

But, 'Let's go,' they said, and we went to Tama.

Tamatekapua. I sat beside a cabinet minister who came from the same town at dinner the other night. 'I used to go to Tama,' I said, giving him a sly look between dessert and coffee. 'So did I,' he said, 'yes, do you remember the steak and eggs for supper? Oh yes, *those were the days.*'

We took off our shoes to enter the meeting house. Outside, the air was thick with sulphur fumes, inside the smoke was so thick you could hardly see the other end from the door. The lights were always low in Tama. Sometimes they jerked and died altogether. Bodies flew beside the tukutuku panels, feet stamped out a rhythm, the blind saxophone player Tai Paul's music rippled up and down at the front of the small platform where the band played. To one side of Tai Paul, a young man with his hair slicked back was singing his heart out; his name was Howard Morrison.

'Heavenly shades of night are falling / It's twilight time / Deep in the dark your kiss will thrill me / It's twilight time . . .' Yes, Howard

baby, now that's a song. And over in the corner, I get to see Johnnie Gin and her man who is also called Howie: he tosses her around his waist, his hand flips her over, her legs swing straight out, feet connect with the ground, his feet slide apart, her body shoots through them like an arrow, his fingers release her as she springs back up again, they weave apart, she waggles her fingers in the air, holds them to the corner of her eyes, and pulls them out straight at him, although they are very round and wide.

I went over to her. She didn't smile. 'How're you going?' I asked her.

'Okay. You having a good time then?' She flicked her head in the direction of the others.

'Yeah, okay.'

'Hear you're going to be a beauty queen?'

'Eh? Oh I dunno.'

I offered her a smoke. She took it but she didn't look as if she was enjoying our conversation.

The others seemed to be just standing around. I can hear those men now, Miles and Bozo anyway. I'll bet they say, that place had atmosphere.

After a while Smitty began to dance with me. He danced as if he was playing basketball. Then the others started dancing, and soon I was with Bozo again.

The summer streets of our small provincial town. It is a city now but when I pass through it I see the same things I saw then, even if some of them are gone. It is a town that has been full of hotels as long as living memory. Prince's Gate still stands but the Grand has gone, an immense, elegant, pale grey building, now burned to the ground. The Palace was bright pink, it is 'tidied up' now. The railway station used to be approached by an avenue of trees; now no trains come and the buildings are concrete block afflicted by graffiti.

I watched the New Year's Eve Parade. The library closed for half an hour. There was a long open verandah down one side of the building, which was reached through glass doors opening onto it. A wide garden edged it, dense with dark lobelia and petunias this year. The librarian sat by the garden and read while the procession was on. She wore a wide sunhat and a cool blue

15

linen dress. She pretended that the parade was not happening. Allowing us to shut was her only concession to our vulgarity. It was pointless to stay open, she remarked each year, the borrowers cannot get through the crowds. She never said that it was because nobody would come.

The procession of floats wound through the streets: Scouts in uniform, small girls in their tutus, pipers and marching girls.

The winner of the waitresses' derby (the one who had run the course without spilling a drop from her jug) was hoisted on the hotel float, the biggest and most colourful of them all, wreathed all over with green sidings and pink paper blossoms as if spring had had a late flowering.

The Summer Queen was wearing a dazzling organza dress, layers upon layers of material sprinkled with glitter billowing across the back of the float. She wore a sash across her breast, and she waved her arm above her head to us.

'Well that's the competition,' a voice behind me said. Cliff Parker was young then, a little spindly, with wide luminescent eyes and a way of jabbing his head towards you. He was the film projectionist in the theatre which shared the same building as the library.

I realised with a perspicacity that alarmed me that the Summer Queen would indeed be my rival when I paraded as Miss Blue Lake.

If I did.

The crowd pressed against me, reeking of hot dogs and candy floss. A hurdy-gurdy played a tinkling tune.

'Who told you?' I said foolishly, although it had become clear that half the town knew. I fancied that even some of the borrowers looked at me in a curious fashion, as if I was not wearing clothes. I stamped books with trembling hands these days.

Cliff was grinning with delight. 'You might get into the movies,' he said.

'I haven't said I'll do it.'

'You'd be mad if you didn't. Don't you want to be famous?'

I said I was still thinking about it. He shook his head.

Afterwards I thought about what he had said and wondered what I did want to make of myself. A firm, lightly tanned young matron I supposed, with a toddler walking on reins and another child lying in a pram dressed in fluffy yellow rompers. I would own a house somewhere. I would buy things in the shops.

Or I would be a librarian until I grew old. I would mend books. I would keep the stackroom in order. The skin round my eyes would grow puffy from reading books. Yes, I would read books.

In the afternoon on the day following New Year I went with Smitty and Miles and Bozo and Linda and Sugar to the lake. We had been up until late the night before. We tired easily: of oiling each other's bodies, of singing little snatches of songs *pretend you're happy when you're blue*, of talking *it isn't very hard to do-o*, of each other. They asked me if I was going to be Miss Blue Lake. Frank had rung Sugar in the morning to ask her. Ask *her*, she had said, meaning me. What's her phone number, he inquired. She told him that I didn't have one. She told me I had better make up my mind, because soon Frank might change his. I knew she meant he thought it was queer the way I didn't have a phone at my house.

She mentioned that everyone was getting sick of me thinking about my decision, as if it were *all that important*. As the afternoon wore on she and Linda offered opinions to each other on a variety of topics as we lay and toasted in a sultry sun; they didn't ask mine about any of them.

Night began to fall, the sun dropped hurriedly away, the air seemed to clear, and a delicate half-light closed in. A ruffle of wind passed over the lake, the last water-skiers went home. We shivered, put on jerseys, talked of going to town to buy fish and chips.

Miles and Linda stood up and said they were going for a walk. Sugar said to Smitty why didn't they, and Bozo and I were left. When he suggested that we go for a walk too I dutifully agreed. Bozo had had his hand on my knee and around my shoulders in the car, which I understood to be a price that must be paid for this passing summer. Linda was engaged; I hadn't been sure how she paid her dues, now I could see the price tag, though I saw too, as she went away with Miles, that it wasn't a hardship.

Bush fronds leaned against the place where Bozo led me; pongas with dark curled hearts touched my face. I lay down in the ferns and put my arms around him. He leaned his face on mine, a little furry like the plants.

'I don't want to do it,' I said.

'Go on, I've brought some joeys.'

17

'No,' I said, 'they affect me.'

'You don't want to do it without?' he muttered.

'No. I don't want to do it.'

He rolled on his back, his face agonised. 'I'll tell them we did it,' I said, divining the true cause of his distress.

'Yeah? Would you?'

'Yes. I'll tell them, that it was, you know, it was nice.'

'You're a good kid. Yeah. You're okay,' he said. We sat smoking Craven A and I heard the bushes crackling. Bozo jumped to his feet, laughing loudly at the sky. A fleck of stars had appeared.

'We're through,' he cried, and Smitty appeared between the trees.

'All yours,' he said, and scurried away, leaving me with Smitty, the graceful basketballer with the sinewy body. He lay down beside me.

'We're taking turns,' he said.

I lay still on the hard ground. In the dim light I saw that others had been there before us. A joey, a cigarette pack, some toffee papers. Smitty put his arm around me in a careless gentle embrace. I liked his warmth, his smell, though I knew it was partly of Sugar: maybe I liked the smell of her. Her body was beautiful to oil.

He rolled towards me, his hands travelled over me.

After a while he sighed, moved away. 'You've got a beautiful body,' he said, 'really beautiful, you don't need to show it to anyone.'

'Honestly?' I wanted to talk to him about the beauty contest; I thought I was on the point of learning something.

Only Miles came then, because it was his turn.

I saw Sugar on my way to work, after the holiday. Linda's fiancé was back, she said, and this afternoon she and Linda planned to finish work early and shop for material for the wedding dresses. They'd decided on guipure lace.

I said that was nice, perhaps I would see them later. Not so, Sugar thought, and her face was serious, embarrassed. Linda's fiancé didn't approve of me, she said, he'd heard I was cheap. It was a pity, but it wasn't her fault. She guessed she would see me round sometime.

Stiffly, I mentioned the contest.

'Oh that,' she shrugged. 'It doesn't really matter.'

18

'You asked me. Frank asked me.'

'I expect they'll find someone.'

I resolved to ring Frank from the library phone in the tea break that afternoon and tell him I would be Miss Blue Lake. When I rang he was out for the day.

At the end of the library was a museum. Part of our duties was to take daily turns at dusting the artefacts each morning and to collect money from people who wished to examine the exhibits. Locals who held cards for the library were admitted free; it cost visitors one shilling.

Few people came in the summer, although in the winter tourists sometimes took shelter there for an hour or so. The room was very dark; in its gloom, under the light of bare electric bulbs, long glass cases contained greenstone adzes and hundreds of pieces of kauri gum. The gum had been liquefied then poured into shapes over objects and creatures and left to set. Spiders and bush wetas and the photographs of gum diggers' dead mothers were entrapped in the dull amber-gold mounds.

I dusted the cases with care. It was easier than shelving books and besides, everything we did in the library was observed by the beautiful woman in charge. She was quick to record our shortcomings.

On this morning I took longer than usual, though I didn't know why we should bother with the room at all. We had taken three shillings the day before. I put my hands on one of the cases and stared through the glass. I felt heavy and tired as if I had slept badly, although I couldn't remember being awake in the night.

'There is work to be done in the library,' the librarian said.

'Yes,' I said, starting. I made as if to go, but she walked over to me, holding me in her intense blue look.

She looked down into the glass case too. The body of a centipede was stretched before us in a lump of resin. She sighed.

'What are you going to do?' she asked.

'About what?' I asked foolishly, although I knew at once that she too must have heard about the bathing beauty contest.

She didn't look at me but continued to gaze at the centipede, captured forever in an ungainly pose.

'I will not have my staff making themselves ridiculous,' she said.

I said nothing. I watched dust motes dance in front of the slit

19

windows of the museum where a little morning sun was filtering through.

'We must improve this room,' she said, looking around her, as if forced to pay attention for once to the part of the building which least interested her.

'Yes. Perhaps we could ask the council for a grant,' I replied.

She nodded and her finely manicured fingers tapped on the glass.

'You'll do well enough,' she said. 'But not at that. You cannot parade yourself in front of people. You cannot do that.'

'You're mad,' Cliff Parker said, when I told him that evening. 'Think of the movies.'

Cliff is like that, a person stepped straight out of his own dramas. I suppose we are all the same.

'It's all right,' I said. 'It's just as well. I can't water-ski, you know.'

'Oh well, there must be something you can do,' he said, with the sort of confidence which has made me remember him. I knew that when I saw him next he would have thought of some other scheme to help me get through life.

'Oh sure there is,' I said, and to reassure him, I added, 'It's a matter of balance. Water-skiing. I could get on my feet next summer.'

I saw waitresses laughing on the balconies of the hotels, a man from the carnival walked through the street holding a plaster head on a stick. The green trees stooped towards the pavement. An eddy of wind tumbled down Fenton Street and a newspaper lifted on this lazy breeze and wrapped itself with sudden vigour around a lamp post and collapsed again. In the evening the long street was as blue as larkspurs. I stopped in front of a shop window and looked down at a pair of red shoes. Just you wait, I thought.

A Moving Life

At five o'clock Anita woke up again and, moving very quietly so as not to disturb her husband, she got out of bed and went to the telephone to ring the taped meteorological service. She was due to fly to Auckland at eight-thirty. The ostensible, and to some extent the actual reason for her flight was in order to attend the meeting of a cultural organisation of which she was a national administrator. Anita wanted to be as sure as it was possible that the planes would be flying, that the weather would permit them to take off. Her fear was almost certainly irrational for the previous evening the sky had only been mildly cloudy. But it was an erratic climate where they lived.

The telephone was in the kitchen, but there was an extension beside their bed. When she dialled there would be a small prickling buzz on the bedroom phone. Brian slept more heavily than she did in the mornings, yet she was so afraid that he would be wakened that her hands shook and her clumsiness seemed to echo through the house.

The voice at the other end was bland and reassuring. She had no doubt that it would have conveyed equal reassurance if there were to be gales or thunderstorms. Because she was in love with a man who lived in Auckland she would brave storms, she would make rash and foolish pacts with destiny, if only she was given the chance to try her luck. It was when chance failed her that she despaired. Nobody would ever know the risks she had taken in the name of love, or how foolish some of them had appeared to her when she remembered them later. As she replaced the receiver it occurred to her that fine weather did not necessarily mean the absence of fog, and that on an otherwise perfect day a funnel of vapour might roll off the sea and cover the airport. Where they lived it had been known to happen, sometimes for days on end.

She walked to the window then, cautious so that she would not catch the loose floorboard. Sometimes she had walked on it in the night, making a sound like gunshot. Or so it always seemed. Her life was much preoccupied with how things seemed.

This morning as she bathed and dressed to go to the airport she must seem to Brian as if the event was of little importance. Interesting, yes; fraught with the slight edge of panic which always accompanied either of them when they flew, yes — that too. But not crucial to her wellbeing. No, she must not allow that to show. She was, after all, only flying to Auckland for a short meeting. It would be over in an hour or two, and tonight she would be back here and they would be going out to dinner. Though she couldn't remember why they had agreed on a week night. Their friends must have better organised lives and a greater resilience to hangovers than she did. Brian pointed out that she didn't have to get a hangover, that it was not essential to a night out, and that they were falling into some kind of trap that insisted on this ritual suffering. Yet when it came to the point on these occasions, he too would invariably look ill the next morning, his face gleaming with an unnatural pallor while it was still sleek from shaving.

She had said that she could find her own way to the airport, but he would have none of it. He called to her to hurry when she was still halfway through her make-up. Her face stared back at her from the glass, the shadows under her eyes smoky and huge. She had hardly slept at all. Or, again, so it seemed. She had read recently that people who thought they lay awake at nights often did so only for a few minutes or even seconds, believing it to be hours. But that had not been the case last night. She had listened to Brian's even breathing, the occasional snore as he rolled over, felt his arm flung over her from time to time. He had rolled eight times while she was awake and put his arm around her three times. That was not imagination, or the passage of seconds. That was a long time. The last time he had rolled against her he had had an erection in his sleep. That was when she moved carefully away from him and got up. And she hadn't slept since then. When she got back into bed he had been asleep again. Almost unnaturally so, as if it were just possible that he was feigning. To test him she had lain along the length of his back and slid her hand down this thigh. He had continued to sleep and she believed that he had not heard her phone call. But she did not sleep again.

Her reddish-brown hair fizzed around her face. She had high bones in her face and she was more gaunt than was generally considered attractive. She wore little make-up as if to emphasise that it didn't matter whether she was good-looking or not and, being tall, expected few people to analyse her appearance. Anita was a presence, and she was intelligent. It was this which mattered, to show an intelligent face to the world. But this morning the stretched lines and smudges invited more attention to detail. She was still working at it with care when Brian called for the second time. She dragged a comb through the tangle of her hair and gave up. If it was a good flight she could sleep for half an hour on the plane. Which it would be, for the weather was up to its prediction and the sky high and blue beyond the house, now that the day had broken. She wondered how she had managed to be so late when she had been up so early. Yet, oddly, and for no reason that she could explain to herself, she began to put off leaving the house.

'Is Simon out of bed?' she called from the bathroom.

'That's his problem,' said Brian.

'Haven't you called him?'

'I thought you had.'

'I thought you would. You know I'm going away.'

She said 'going away' with an inflection, as if she was leaving them for months.

'I'm tired of running after him as if he was a child,' Brian said, as she appeared in the sitting room.

He was running his hand over a blue vase, a deep glowing blue pot with a perfect orb in its base. 'I like this. Where did you say you got it?'

She didn't reply to that, but said instead, as if speaking of their son, 'What would you all do without me to run after you?' She had banged on Simon's door as she walked through the passage.

'The others managed all right. In the long run,' said Brian.

She supposed they had, although their younger daughter was causing them concern at university — perhaps Caroline would get her degree eventually, though they could all agree that it should have happened sooner, and they didn't like the man the elder one was living with, although Jane continued to behave as if there was nothing wrong and brought him to the house too often, which was almost worse than not seeing her at all.

Simon appeared in the doorway. His face was puffy under a mat of soft down. Anita wanted to touch him then, to cradle him if she could. He had always been the one she most liked to hold. That was how she put it to herself, although what she meant in a secret furtive way, was that he was her favourite child.

'Hasn't anyone at school told you to shave yet?' she heard herself saying waspishly.

He ignored the question. He was good at turning the subject away from himself with a simple refusal to answer. Like her.

'I'm going away,' she said.

'Oh yeah, what did you wake me up for?'

'School. Remember? The house of learning.'

'I've got study leave. Have you forgotten?'

She had. He had told her the night before, chatty and amiable while she was preparing dinner, the sort of moment she enjoyed with him.

'I mean . . .' She faltered. 'If you don't get up you'll have wasted your day. You won't get any study done.'

He turned on her, shouting. 'Shove off and leave me alone.' His voice broke on the end of his words, so that they turned to a scream.

Anita picked up her coat and threw it over her arm, reaching for her briefcase. 'We'd better hurry,' she said to Brian.

'I've been telling you that for ten minutes.'

'Where are you going?' Simon asked as she walked out the door.

'I told you. Have you forgotten?' She closed the door behind her, hating her cheap parting shot.

In the car Brian said, 'Why don't you start potting again?'

'I don't have the time,' she said. 'Anyway, I don't think I'm much good. I don't know that I ever have been.'

'Does that matter?'

'It's all very well being in these organisations, and running things, but if you don't do it yourself . . .' He shrugged.

'I do a good job. It's a useful way to earn my keep.'

'Administration. It's not the same as doing it yourself, that's all.'

'That's rich. Coming from you.' She knew they were close to some kind of quarrel, the kind that she suppressed these days. The sort that on no account she wanted to have before she boarded the plane this morning.

'That's different. I'm a trained administrator. That's all I know how to do. As you know.'

'A trained public servant.' She gazed away from him out the window, watching the coastline as they passed it.

'If you like. But at least I know what I am.'

'I'm not a trained anything,' she said. 'I do the best I can. You know what that means, picking up here and there.'

'You don't know whether you're a good potter or not,' he insisted. 'You never gave it a fair try. The kiln, your shed, all the equipment, you don't use it any more . . . You don't have to be the best, do you?'

Her hands, lying in her lap, looked large and heavy-knuckled to her. She turned them over, and wondered if they could make things or not. In her head she always could, but when she really tried to do certain things they didn't satisfy her, were never as good as she hoped. Secretly, she knew that it was the best that she wanted, that it was perfection itself that was out of her grasp. Love and art were inextricably twined. They were one and the same. Their pursuit was a common goal. Somehow she could never get quite near enough.

He turned his attention to the traffic, and it was banked up at the intersection. As she glanced at her watch she saw that it was close to check-in.

'I'll get you there on time. I told you we should have left earlier.' His voice was weary and slanted with anger.

'I didn't ask you to bring me.'

They continued in silence, Brian accelerating through the traffic at speed now. Outside the terminal building he said, 'What time am I picking you up?'

'Don't worry, I'll find my own way home.'

He sighed, clenching his jaw over the need to be held responsible for her. 'What time are we due at the Corbetts' for dinner, then?'

'Oh . . . sevenish, seven-thirty.' As she closed the door she relented. 'My plane's due at six.' She remembered that Ellen was cooking Italian these days. Brian had never cared for pasta.

In the queue at the check-in counter a television interviewer whom Anita and Brian had met with her husband at a dinner party was arguing with a Government Member of Parliament. The interviewer had sharp yellow hair and was wearing a Stetson with green feathers in the band.

She said, 'I do love you, you know.'

'You love power,' the politician said, as if it was a revelation.

'You say that to me?' Her voice was rising on a dangerous note.

'Keep your voice down. Please.'

She smiled. She had beautiful glittering teeth. 'I could bring the Government down, you know.'

They moved forward and collected their seat numbers. Anita found they had got the last non-smoking seats.

When she was seated on the plane she realised she was shaking. She strapped herself in and accepted a magazine, starting at once to read an article about de Lorean. The rise and fall of a man. His wife appeared beautiful in her photographs. To say nothing then of the fall of a woman. The pilot announced that due to mechanical fault in the plane they would not take off. In fact, they would actually have to get off the plane and wait for another one to arrive from somewhere else. Or they might have to be re-ticketed on to other flights. The yellow-haired interviewer was crying when they got off the plane. Her mascara was collecting in the otherwise indiscernible folds under her eyes. The sea shone with blinding azure clarity to the side of the runway as they all walked off the tarmac.

It was ten-thirty when the flight took off, which meant that by the time they landed and she had made her way into town, Anita's meeting would be almost over. She knew that she had no right to be on the plane. Her mind revolved around ways of paying for her own flight and refunding the money for the ticket while at the same time explaining to Brian, or her colleagues, or whoever might care, why she had gone ahead with the flight anyway. At the airport, as she waited, she had been similarly confused. She could not decide whether she should ring the committee and tell them that she was unable to make it to the meeting, so that they were not expecting her in Auckland even though she still intended to go. Then she was afraid that if she did, someone (anyone, Brian, one of the children, her office in town) might ring with messages and find that she had not left — or appeared not to have gone. Or, when she arrived in Auckland, that some disaster might befall the evening flight so that she could not return, and that too would reveal her deceptions. And so on. She had read stories like that. And she had once had a lover who imagined earthquakes when they were in hotel rooms, car accidents when they went on a picnic, and worst, that they might be caught in a street scene by a television camera and shown on the news together to the whole country that night. She had loved him with a passion so intense that she recalled once standing gazing out to sea at dawn and thinking of him and being certain that every day for the rest of her life she would wake thinking of him. Now she remembered that

moment more clearly than she could recollect his face.
Yet for a time his fears had infected her. Now, although he belonged so far in her past, she recognised his mark.

In the end she did nothing. It would be easier to plead ignorance of times, or show zealous concern for an arrival, even a late one, than to invent excuses. Her colleagues would be displeased but they would understand. Anita has ideas, they would say, but she doesn't think ahead. And Brian knew that she was good at buying lettuces and detergents but never remembered to buy theatre tickets until a show was booked out. In a situation like this he would have hoped she would do better, of course.

There were no taxis when they landed. The television interviewer took the last one. The politician had already left the airport building by the time the woman walked through and claimed the taxi. Anita ran after her, making little gasping noises to attract her attention and couldn't remember her name to call out to her. She should have paid more attention and taken note of who she was. On screen, in the den where they watched television, she would have summoned her name as easily as those of her children.

She took the bus rather than wait for the stand to fill again. In the city, Conrad, the man she was in love with now, would be gathering up his papers and books after delivering his last lecture for the morning, and returning to his office to put them away before he set off to meet her.

She stared out the window across the flat sad waterway of Mangere. She had read in the paper, not long ago, that someone had staked a dog up in the scrub that jutted out there into the water where the tide came in. The dog was very thin when it was discovered and near to death. It was thought that the tide had covered it many times, and that each time it had survived by reaching its nose up just above the waterline until the tide receded. After it was released it died. Anita wondered what the significance of that was. Freedom is death. Huh. Deeply aware political statement, Ma, as Jane would have said when she first went to university, and before she met her boyfriend.

Anita and Conrad ate their meal too fast and she drank more than she had intended. He had been annoyed that in the end she had kept him waiting while she made phone calls to explain her absence from the meeting and exaggerated the difficulties (making it sound as if she had been trapped aboard a stationary aircraft on the tarmac, which was not a bad story, really quite credible, and had only occurred to her as she dialled), smoothed things over and salvaged something of the meeting by agreeing to call in and go through the rough draft minutes, which would be ready at four. This meant that she would have to catch a later plane, so that then she had to ring Brian to explain what had happened (or what by now she believed had happened), and that she would be a bit late but it didn't matter if they didn't make it to the Corbetts' until eight. He responded easily, as if she was at home and they hadn't been sharp with each as they parted, asking her what the temperature was up there, and if it was today that he had seen a dentist appointment written up on the kitchen calendar for Simon, and if so should he ring to remind him, also had she remembered that there was an office party for Mollie Levett's retirement on Friday, and would he say that she was coming? She was standing in an open phone booth at Downtown with Conrad standing beside her; she was stretching towards some terrible point of tension, trying to match Brian's comfortable voice, yet aware of Conrad's increasing anger, and of the appalling, overwhelming strength of her desire for him.

'Where will we go?' she asked Conrad. His hair was floppy and soft, but styled so that the grey fell evenly in line with his cheekbone. Anita wanted to reach out and stroke his bones with the back of her crooked finger but they were in a smart fast-moving seafood restaurant where many people knew him. The fish was freshly caught and the wine light and pleasant. They were near the waterfront, filtered light spilled through the branches of a tree that had been preserved in the midst of the city. Its branches scraped against the window.

Conrad looked at his watch. 'What do you want to do?'

Even without replying, Anita had an unpleasant feeling that she had been caught begging.

'Well?' He smoked too carefully. He knew she hated smoking, usually didn't when when he was with her, and always cleaned his teeth before they made love. Once he had used her toothbrush. At the time she saw it as some ultimate act of love.

She leaned forward, pushing aside the unfinished plate of flounder. 'I. . . .' It was a whole sentence.

'Yes?'

'It's been five months,' she whispered.

He had been telling her gossip about the university. Some of it had been funny, some malicious. It was like a slightly more spicy summary of one of Brian's days at the office. He had brought her a book of poems as a gift. He always brought her a gift. Last time it had been the dark blue pottery vase. She had kept it filled with flowers during the summer.

'Yes,' he agreed, stubbing out his cigarette. 'Pity we couldn't do something about it. Went through my mind — nice if we could. Pretty hopeless when you're not staying.'

'I couldn't. Not this time. But I had to . . . I don't know when I'll get up again. It's all gone wrong. I'm sorry.' She didn't know why she apologised, only that she was profoundly tired, and she recalled how little sleep she had had.

'Perhaps we could take a drive somewhere?' Anita said.

He gave a slight smile. 'Not quite our style, is it? Long grass and all that sort of thing. Look, I've got a lecture at three, I'll have to be heading back soon. Can I drop you off?'

'Thank you, Conrad.' Her voice was faint.

In the car she asked him to stop. They were on an incline in a small back street. The only place to park was between two sets of workmen. She reached out her hand so that he took it as of habit; the habit of taking a woman's hand rather than of taking hers.

'I don't know when I'll see you again,' she said.

'Oh we'll sort something out. Take it as it comes,' he said.

'You do want to see me again then?'

He scratched his head with his little finger and smiled. 'Well of course I do. You get too upset.'

'I wanted you. I mean, I want you. Now.'

'I know. But it's too fast, too rushed. What good will that do us?'

She wanted to tell him that it was everything but instead she said, 'I want to tell you something. It's got nothing to do with you, but I thought that if you heard . . . well, you might think it was strange if I hadn't told you.'

'Try me.'

'I'm thinking of leaving. Leaving home, that is. I mean, well, Brian of course.'

A workman peered into the car. In a moment he would ask

Conrad to move the car on, as they shifted their drilling down the street.

'You'll find it pretty lonely,' Conrad said. He had once left his wife for a while, before he met Anita.

'I could bear it,' she said.

'You don't know for sure until you try.'

'Wouldn't you ever do it again?' She regretted asking him immediately.

'Never,' he said, as she expected.

They were silent. A pneumatic drill started close by.

'It's got nothing to do with you,' said Anita again. 'I just thought you should know.'

His eyes flicked down to his watch again. He drummed his fingers on the steering wheel and she could see he was planning how to get out of the spot they were in without running over any of the square-cut gashes in the street's sealing.

'Well. Thanks. Yes, I'm pleased you told me.'

'I haven't absolutely decided yet. But, that I'm thinking of it, you see?'

'Well you should think it through, that's right. I mean, you really should.' His voice held a touch of melancholy now. Once he had been a chorister.

'I'd better get going, then,' Anita said.

'Always on the move, aren't you?' he said, flattering her. He eased the car round the roped-off section of the road and down towards Queen Street.

'That's what it's all about.' She sounded so bright and efficient that she thought it unfortunate that she had not been at the meeting after all. 'Keeping on the move, that's what I like.' He had stopped at a set of lights and she prepared to slide out of the car.

'Good of you to let me know you were in town. Take care,' he called, his voice expressing urgency as the traffic around them began to move.

He missed the change and she had to stand on the edge of the street waiting for a pedestrian signal while he, at the same time, sat waiting for the traffic to flow in his direction again. They exchanged small smiles and waves, and she wished that he would disappear. After a time the lights changed in his favour.

She had never had a flight quite like this before. The plane appeared to follow the sinking sun and then small clouds picked up a bright crimson glow, a reflection from objects at the level of the earth or the sea. She saw that it was the oil rigs standing off the Taranaki coastline, flaming turrets abroad on the water.

It occurred to Anita that men had never been much attracted to her. But that was self-pitying and not true. Men had been tremendously, overwhelmingly attracted to her, had pursued her with great sexual ardour. It was the strength of her responses that invariably turned them away in the end. When she was much younger her mother and her aunts advised her against wearing her heart on her sleeve. That was what they called it. Your heart on your sleeve, as if a great pulsing organ could be safety-pinned to the arm of her cousin's hand-me-down dyed forest-green flannel coat that she wore in winter over her dance frock when she went out to meet boys.

What they really meant was that they would never wear their faces bare as she did, never show their true selves unadorned. They had designed reserves in which they could shelter and never be altogether found. This was something Anita had not learned or discovered, how to fashion a disguise for her naked-ness or her greed. So much pain and foolishness in the name of love. Or what sometimes passed as love.

The politician was on the half-empty plane. The television interviewer was not. From the headlines in the evening paper Anita deduced that the Government remained intact. She opened her briefcase as if to work, but it was a gesture. The case was a beautiful burgundy leather one which Brian had bought her overseas. Inside, it contained two sheets of blank paper, a spare pair of clean panties, her toothbrush and the new book of poems. She thought about weeping but remembered in time that they were going to the Corbetts'. She hoped that Ellen would not be too late with her dishes of antipasto and pasta, aubergine, olives and sauces. She hoped that there would be a lot of wine, and then she hoped that there would not.

Bunches of stars appeared in the still not-quite-dark sky, close to the wingtip of the plane. They seemed to move. Seemed. Within the plane she felt stationary, as if it was the stars rather than her that were being propelled. Up here, above the earth, she was for a moment less sorry than usual that she behaved as she did.

At the airport Brian said, 'So the weather did stay fine all day.' She saw that his hair needed cutting.

There He Comes

Vroom. And there he comes again out of a cineraria-coloured sky, a blue so hot it burned you in the eye, full of purples and greens reflected out of the sea, and the day hardly open for inspection. Vroom . . .

Erik steps into the kitchen and the morning is a lake. He must break its surface. He wishes Margo would talk to him more but she has had little to say since he stepped off the plane. He reminds himself that it is still only seven-thirty.

She stands at the bench now, resurrecting coffee. It is probably last night's for there is not even a lingering smell of fresh grounds in the air. It is her coffee, from another life that did not include him, made when he was somewhere over the Pacific, coming home.

He considers the room with care, as if replacing everything. But of course it is not the room that has moved, it is him, it is he who must familiarise again. There is a friendly disorder in the room, a clutter of vegetables on the end of the bench as if Margo has not put away all the shopping from the day before. It flits through his mind that once, in the days when he first went to conferences and they were younger . . . when they were young, he corrects himself, everything would have been in place for his return, and there would have been fresh coffee. He is vaguely irritated by papers on the table, by a small rime of the filmy dust that collects and coagulates in kitchens on the red bowl-shaped lamp hanging over the breakfast recess. Margo has help in the house, there is no call for it. But then he reminds himself that he is tired of hotel rooms and the sharp smell of antiseptic as he wakes. It is to this that he has been looking forward.

Margo turns towards him. Her skin has a slightly floury look and there are smudges under her eyes. With love, he remembers that she has been up since four-thirty and that she has already had an hour's drive to the airport and then all the way back again.

Her loom stands in the next room. Through the glass panel he sees that she has been working. There is a new piece on the frame.

'Been working?' he comments.

'I've got my exhibition soon,' she says evenly.

'Of course.' It's too late to pretend he had remembered.

She is holding her coffee, makes to sit down beside him, sees that he is reaching for the pile of papers, and turns towards the balcony.

'Why don't we sit outside?'

He guesses that there are bills in the pile. He sighs. There are always bills. If he asks to go through them with her, she will, with exaggerated patience, showing him the savings that have been made and the necessity of certain purchases; remark on how difficult it is with a teenage boy and girl with growing feet, and how you have to buy separately for each of them, it's not as if you can pass things on with a boy and a girl. She will behave like a martyred downtrodden housewife who does not have financial independence of her own, as well as a husband who brings home a large and steady income.

The harbour lies below them, glimpsed through a network of trees, a large Australian eucalypt and a silver birch pushing aside natives they have planted. It is only a month since he went away but it all looks overgrown. As they settle themselves on the slatted benches on the balcony, instead of asking how much their Visa card is overdrawn, he says, 'Hasn't Andrew been doing the lawns and hedges?'

'It's been raining a lot.'

He knows she always defends their son.

'At this time of year?'

'Showers at the weekends. Andy should be up soon.'

'He could have come and got me. It would have saved you.'

'I thought you liked me to come to the airport.'

'I *do*, sweetheart. But you're *tired*. You said so.'

'Well that's what I said, yes I suppose it's true, but it's early . . .'

'That's what I mean.'

'He's too young, he's only just got his licence.'

'Well, yes, but I mean, he has *got* it. I mean either he's old enough to have a licence or he's not, if he can't use it for something useful, something to help you, I mean for God's sake, that was the idea, not just for his lordship's pleasure . . .'

'I don't have to take him to tennis any more. And the shopping. Well he does do shopping now.'

'Was it him who left the vegetables out last night?'

'Erik!'

'I'm sorry.'

Around them is the vivid sound of morning, leaves scraping on the railings they creosoted together last year, the singing, sighing rasp of insects, the slap of joggers' feet on the road below.

'It was hard to get a park at the airport, that's all,' she says, harking back to her shortness on his arrival. 'You wouldn't think, not at that hour of the morning, would you? I always think, don't you, that it's better to sit and wait for someone to pull out than to drive round and round, but at that hour, nothing much is moving — well I sat for ten minutes. Be patient, I said, you *know* this always works, then I thought it wouldn't. Just when I was getting, like, quite frantic, this man, he's been sitting there all along reading a newspaper and I hadn't noticed, see, he pulls out, and a red Porsche comes whipping up the side of me and tries to steal the park. I nearly rammed him. God, I thought, a Porsche, a new one at that, what would it cost to fix a Porsche if I'd hit him.'

She explains but his attention has wandered. The skin around her left eye is more drawn than round her right eye. He suspects that she needs a new prescription for her glasses. It irritates her if he mentions it. He understands that, it's the sort of thing he is touchy about too. Life has dealt a mean blow to Margo, he thinks, making her face as lined as it is, when the rest of her skin still fits so well.

He would know her body anywhere in the world. Wouldn't he? She sits level with his shoulder. She is smaller than he remembers. Remembers? It has only been a month. Still, when he is away he sometimes thinks of her as larger than she is. All his perceptions of her become unclear at a distance. In strange rooms, from far away, he imagines her in a sauna where there are many women unclothed. He sees the dark steaming room and bodies on benches. Would he really find her if they had their faces turned away from him, or would he have to feel them all, going from woman to woman touching each one in order to decipher the signature of her body? Or would that only confuse him more, would he become drunk with the skin of many women beneath his hands? Porous, greasy, fine, silky, a little dry in the moist air? Ah, now that would be her. Her body is tidy, to be sure, but it is also dry and a little flaky in patches along the spine and beneath the right breast. She sunbathes too much.

He shakes himself. Flying always affects him badly. His head is so light it feels as if he should be holding it in place. His job is so strenuous, so demanding of his concentration when he is away, that it is like abandoning himself on a liferaft when he comes home. He knows he will be saved but in the meantime he feels seasick.

She bends over the coffee cup. At least he would know her toffee-coloured hair anywhere. It is thick and going grey in random streaks, but it is still bright beside his shoulder as she lifts her head now and contemplates the bay.

'Did you have nice secretaries?' she asks.

It is a standard question, started as a joke, but it has developed an edge.

'All right.'

'How many did you sleep with?' She is punishing him still for the vegetables.

'Two or three,' he says, snapping with sudden anger.

'Good,' she says, getting to her feet. 'Good, I hope they enjoyed it.'

'You might hope that I did.'

They glare at each other, her eyes round with a real question now, but she won't ask it.

'Sweetheart, you asked for it.'

'It gets lonely.' She gathers cups with neat correct actions, standing as if she is a waitress clearing his table. He puts his hand out, covering hers.

'You should say, We should talk about it.'

She disengages herself. 'I've got to wake Andy.' Dismissing him.

'Did Ken come over? Do you know if he checked the boat?' Ken is his friend. They own a small launch between them that they fish from together. He is almost certain that Margo and he were lovers once. For a whole painful year she hardly ever heard him when he spoke to her, and she cried in the middle of the night when she thought he was asleep. The children had been very small. Mostly he thought now that he had dreamed it, that either he had never heard her cry, or if she did that she had been tired from the children.

'I think so. Ask the children. I was out a lot.'

She has become brisk, but if there is a change in her it has been an imperceptible shift, indicating that she is in a hurry now.

It is not necessary to call Andy after all. He emerges, tousled, his features thick with sleep.

'What's the time? Why didn't you call me?'

'I went to get your father.' There is a note of warning, and supplication, in her voice.

35

'Oh yeah. Hi. Good trip?'

'Yes. Thank you.'

'Je-*sus*. I'm late, I'm supposed to play squash with Ralph before school.'

'No you're not,' Margo says. 'He rang last night to cancel.'

'Why didn't you tell me?'

'I left a note. You didn't look. I'm not staying up all night to give you messages. Anyway, I had to get up early.' She does not look at Erik.

Andy goes to the fridge and takes out a carton of fruit juice, comes out onto the balcony and straddles a seat beside his father. 'It was okay then, was it?'

'Same as usual. I got you a new camera.'

'Yeah?' His face lights up. At seventeen his son has resigned himself, almost but not quite, to exclusion from the childhood pleasures of coming-home presents.

The camera is a Rolleiflex. He opens it tenderly. 'Jeez. It's um, it's cool. Whaddya get Beulah?'

'Eh. Oh junk, it's in the bag there.' Erik can hardly remember what he had got his daughter at the duty free.

'Where is Beulah?' he asks. 'Shouldn't she be up too?'

'Her school's got a holiday today.'

'What *for*?'

'Uh, recreation day, I don't know. Ask Mum.'

Erik feels his heart breaking. He does not want Beulah home today. He wants to spend the morning with Margo, he needs to sleep and not have to pay attention to either of his children, he hopes that later in the morning when he has rested awhile that he will make love to Margo in daylight by the moving shadows of the ngaio tree outside their room.

In the afternoon he will go into the office.

But Beulah too is up and about. She emerges from her room in a rush, flings herself at her father in an emotional embrace, the first he has had since arriving. She clings to him, and he feels the small tight new breasts under her nightdress pressing against his shirt front. So pretty, he thinks, setting her back a little from him, suddenly self-conscious of her and not wanting her to know. This exquisite dark-haired blue-eyed child is his. She looks like the child of a successful man, he thinks with pride.

'Beulie baby,' he says, 'it's so good to see you. No school today, eh? What are you going to do with yourself?' For he has decided that he isn't going to mind her presence after all.

Her face closes. She shoots a sideways glance at her mother.

'I'm meeting my friends Jenny and Tabatha.'

'No you're not,' says Margo.

'I am, I promised them.' Beulah's voice has shot into high gear. Erik hates it when she whines. It is easy to forget, when he's away, that sweet kids like Beulah can have flaws as well as virtues. He has always thought that she was a demanding child.

'Hey Dad, have you *used* this camera?' Andy's voice is aggrieved.

'Yes, for Customs you know. It has a film in it.'

'Oh . . . well. Yeah.'

'Besides, I wanted to take some photographs of your grand-parents.'

His family glance at each other guiltily. They have forgotten to ask after Erik's parents who live in England. His trips are always extended to see them, even if he goes to the States. The computer world has treated him kindly.

'Gran and Grandfather are well,' he says. 'They send their love. They've sent you some presents.' Nobody asks him what they are and he does not tell them. Margo understands that he must carry home crochet-covered coathangers and knitted tea cosies assembled in a terrace house in London, but the children find it more difficult. It is three years since they last saw these strangers, and it is unlikely that the grandparents will travel here again. Next time it must be the children who travel the distance of the world. If it is not too late.

'Where are you going with those girls?' Margo asks Beulah.

'To the *shopp*-ing centre.'

'Just to the shopping centre? You've got no money to spend at the shopping centre.'

'We're just going to *look*.'

'Hang around. No, you can't go, tell her she can't go, Erik.'

'How do you take the film out, Dad? It's stuck.'

Erik sees that Andy has opened the back of the camera. 'Don't do that.'

'Why not? You gave it to me.'

'It's your grandparents. You've ruined the film. You've spoiled the pictures.' He hears his own voice, fraught like the rest of them, and full of grief. When he said goodbye to his parents at Clapham Station he had thought he would never see them again. He had turned at the entrance to the subway and waved to them. 'Don't come in with me,' he had said. He was surprised they had come this far, usually they farewelled him at the gate as he got into a taxi. This time they had said, let's go for a walk, let's pretend it's long ago, we'll walk across the common with you. Like a farewell without an end. He knew that was what they meant and had been deeply touched. On the common he had taken their pictures, standing, leaning together, into each other, he had thought, with pain. A few minutes afterwards he had kissed his mother, shaken hands with his father, and walked down into the station. He turned back once. They were still standing as he had photographed them, watching as he vanished into the tube.

'It was my parents,' he says.

'I'm sorry.' Andy puts the camera on the table, abandoning his gift, and walks away towards his room. The door closes behind him.

'I don't want to stay here all day,' says Beulah, in her dangerous persisting twelve-year-old voice.

'There are lots of things you can do,' says her mother.

'What? For instance, what?'

'You can have your friends over here for the day.'

'I could go to their place,' says Beulah doubtfully, sensing a compromise.

'But I don't know their mothers,' Margo says.

'They don't know you,' Beulah reminds her.

The phone rings. Beulah throws herself at it, getting there before her mother. The conversation is muted. Erik goes to the bathroom, tired of them. When he returns there is crisis in the air. A rendezvous has been arranged at a bus stop and one girl has already left to meet the others there. Or so Beulah says. What will happen to this girl if her friends are not there to meet her? She has made an ar-*range*-ment.

Margo has agreed that she go. Her face is taut with worry. She looks to Erik but he is drowning in this disaster of a morning.

It is only when the house is empty of children that he realises that none of them have eaten breakfast. He thinks he is disintegrating. His eyes travel over the bills. The Visa account is two thousand overdrawn.

The phone shrills beside him. As he stretches out his hand to pick it up he sees that the American Express is twice as much as he calculated.

'Erik Wicklow speaking.'

On the other end a woman's high hysterical voice holds forth. At first he thinks it must be a wrong number until he begins to unravel what she is saying. 'For you, I think.' He hands the phone to Margo.

Yes, yes, yes, I'm Beulah's mother, they didn't, oh no no, they can't do that, I said, yes, that's what I said, I'll have to think . . . call you back.

Tabatha's mother. The other girl's mother had just called her, wanting to know where Jenny was.

'But isn't that the one who was supposed to be waiting at the bus stop?'

'That's right. It's a set-up. She told *her* mother that she was at Tabatha's for the night. But she wasn't.'

'But wasn't it Jenny who just rang Beulah?'

'Yes.'

'So Beulah knows where . . . oh my God, they're only twelve, these kids.'

'What shall we do?'

'Police.'

'No, not yet. Too heavy.'

My God, he thinks again, all the jargon, but really we don't know a thing, not any one thing at all.

'Go after them then. We must go after them,' he says.

'I will, I know what Tabatha looks like at least. You stay here.'

'What am I supposed to do?'

'Answer the phone. Well somebody has to do that.'

'If you don't find her?' He no longer cares about Tabatha or Jenny, there is only Beulah with long dark hair and a long white smile. Beulah, his daughter.

'Then we'll have to think again.'

Only she does find Beulah, and Tabatha. Together, they had still been on their way to meet Jenny, who had appeared within minutes, and her mother had arrived too, and taken her away.

And Margo has met Tabatha's mother, who turns out to be all right, sensible and nice in fact, and they have decided that it is a time to be positive, not to punish. They will talk to the girls later, when they are at home and calmer. In the meantime, Tabatha's mother has offered to organise a day with the girls, shopping first and then the pictures, if that's all right with Margo. She'll stay with them all day, it's that Jenny, thank God they're not her mother. So it's going to be all right . . .

But she sits with her hands clenched on the table. 'I could kill her, I want to kill her,' she explodes. She half stands, beats her fists up and down. 'D'you hear me, I want to kill her. Is this what it's going to be like?' she cries. And when he doesn't answer, she cries out that it isn't fair, nothing's fair, takes a run towards her loom with the suspended dazzling panel that she is weaving stretched upon it, and makes to turn it over.

Erik catches her by the wrists, expecting the worst. All right now, all right. It's all right.

Her hands drop, her body flattens out, she is suddenly calm. Of course it is, of course.

'It's natural,' he says. 'I was frightened too. I felt helpless. While you were out, I didn't know what to do. Well, I could have killed her too.'

They are entirely reasonable with each other, so understanding. He is glad he was here for her when this happened. How awful if she had had to bear it on her own.

'Come to bed,' he says.

She shakes her head, not yet. He must get some sleep, she has things to do. He hears this as the morning at last closes in and over him, he sinks beneath its weight. He hears Margo say that she is going out again for a short time. Sleep, just sleep. She will be back soon.

When he wakes, the photographs of his parents are propped on the dressing table beside the bed, their faces looking at him across Clapham Common on a bleak February morning in England. It is some kind of miracle.

'Sweetheart, Margo, where are you?' He lies on the bed, demanding her presence in the room, certain of his happiness.

She comes in smiling.

'How?' He gestures towards the photographs.

'I got the chemist to take them out in his darkroom. They were all right. If you'd used all the film the last ones would have been spoiled, but there were still some left.'

'Right. Good thinking. Oh, you're so clever, thank you, come to bed now, huh?' All in a rush, no stopping for finesse, or talking, just the way it's always been, going to bed again, after he's been away.

He cannot, will not, believe she hesitates again. But she slips her thickening ankles out of her sneakers, pulls her blouse off with fingers a little grimy with ingrained dirt, such a fine body though, yes he was right, her breasts have milky-blue veins around the nipples, even now, oh Margo my sweet, here I come. Out of the sky.

He is too quick, he feels her withdraw from him.

'All right? Are you all right?' he asks.

And, yes, she murmurs against his ear, yes, yes, it is all right.

Only, afterwards, he supposes that it is not quite all right, in spite of their effort, their goodwill. He thinks that there is probably no special reason why this should be so. He has no reason to doubt her, less perhaps than she to doubt him. She no longer walks along a green path as she did once (and this once is the only absolute thing he ever had to go on, nothing more) to meet his friend. Perhaps at times she is a trifle rueful, as he is too, for the way they have fought and behaved. She is a little vague, mildly careless, she works hard, is thrifty (yes, even that), she is creative, she is motherly, and she thinks a great deal, maybe all the time. It appears that she is the same.

Yet, in a small isolated space around his heart, he knows she has moved a little way from him, towards some private place of her own. He has always gone on so far ahead. Now he does not know how to follow.

In the stillness of the house he knows that an image has changed.

He can see now, how kindness undoes things. He sees that she has given away the cruelty on which he depended. Once or twice this morning they have come thrillingly close to it, but she has skated away, avoided it. It seems that they must learn to live without savagery.

The Whiteness

When it is Easter Sunday somewhere in the world but not in the country where you are, a mile down into the ravine at Samaria does not seem a bad place to contemplate one's spirituality.

Or for that matter, one's mortality. The Samaria Gorge is the longest and deepest in the world, running between the White Mountains. To get to the Mountains one must go by bus, then for those who are fit enough there is a walk through the Gorge, a distance of nine miles. The traveller who makes this walk emerges on the other side of Crete to catch a boat back to Chania.

That is not possible all through the year, because of snow in the winter, or, in the spring when I was there, melting snows can cause flash floods in the Gorge. If you begin to go down and then find that the way is impassable, there is only one way to leave, and that is by the way you came, back up the rough mountain path.

The sign at the bus depot said that the Gorge was closed, but the woman who sold the tickets said that it was open. She wanted me to buy a ticket for the entire journey. I pointed to the sign and she laughed. There were young Germans with blond hair and flashing white teeth waiting in the queue. They were wearing mountain boots and they were impatient to buy their tickets. I looked at their boots and asked the woman about my shoes.

She did not understand. I took off my soft slip-on sneaker and held it up. Was it suitable? She laughed again, and took off one of her own shoes, a little high-heeled pump. She shook her head at her own shoe — *ochi*, no. She clicked her teeth with disapproval at her offending footwear. Then she nodded at mine. '*Endaxi*. Okay. Understand?'

The Germans were muttering to each other. I bought my ticket and boarded the bus.

In the Mountains I looked for a guide, but there was none. When you go into Samaria you are on your own. I think that that is as it should be. The silence of the mountains becomes your own silence. Each decision you make belongs only to you.

What you can, or cannot, or will not endure becomes something for which you are responsible.

It may be that you will make the wrong decision in the mountains and then I believe it would be possible to die. But this would have been your mistake, an inability to judge elements and your capabilities in the face of them.

Oh well, yes, you may say, that is all very well, that is what mountaineers and white water rafters and adventurers of one kind or another do all the time.

That is so, but theirs is a calculated risk, a knowledgeable gamble; they are not tourists thrown suddenly and unexpectedly for a day into a primitive wilderness.

I do not pretend that I was anything else. 'Dear little Ellen,' murmured the English woman in the bar, the night before, 'do go, I'm sure you will love Samaria.' She and her husband claimed they knew I was a New Zealander the moment I opened my mouth but I did not believe them, for they did not say so until I told her from where I came. We may recognise each other's curious flat vowels but Londoners who visit the same place each year, year in and year out (even Chania), and read important literary works as they sit beside the window looking into the bay where the fisherman lifts his lines by night flares, do not know about us. I do not think they know much about anything.

They thought I would not go to Samaria. They had smiled at each other in the way of people who know better. I nearly didn't go, because of them.

Two miles or more down into the Gorge, there is a tiny monastery. If I get as far as that, I said to myself, I will have done well.

For, although it is good to be alone in the mountains, there was also a confusion in the air that day. Certainly there is an aloneness of spirit there, but it would be untrue to suggest that I didn't encounter any other human beings. I had not gone very far along the path when I began to meet people who were coming back up it. They had begun earlier in the day. Nobody seemed to be certain whether the Gorge was open or not, and while some (people who, like the Germans, were wearing heavy boots) had gone on and not returned, others who were already tired just from going down were beginning to understand the enormity, the distance, the sheer climb back that would be entailed if they kept going and then found the Gorge impassable. Some had gone too far, and quite young people were coming back, their faces contorted with distress. It seemed impossible that some of the old ones would ever get back.

I said to a young woman, who was crawling back — this is true, the heat of the day had come upon the mountain, and she would walk a few feet forward then fall on her knees on the jagged path and crawl a short painful way — 'How far did you go?'

She looked at me with glazed eyes, and said, 'Don't go any further, for God's sake, don't go on.'

So that when she and her companions had gone, I sat down in the White Mountains, and I looked at the way that I had come and the way that there was to go, and I thought that I could die in the Mountains if I carried on to the monastery. Sometimes on this journey I had wondered if I would ever reach home again, sometimes I had been afraid. I had left home believing that I was a self-contained person. I was not certain any more. I was often lonely. Other days I felt ill. I am forty-five and my health is no better and no worse than that of many women of my age whose bones are beginning to feel the edge of change.

In the White Mountains I was not afraid, or lonely, or sick. I did not feel that I had to challenge myself to some limit beyond my endurance. The choice was simple which is not to say that the route back was. The heat was pouring between the rocks and midday came and passed and still I climbed back the way I had come. But I would not die in the mountains, I would return from them, and go on.

At two o'clock in the afternoon, at the top of the ravine, there are not too many places to turn. A canteen, and a rest house where a considerable crowd of tourists milled around knowing each other, and that was all.

And no transport until six o'clock that night.

I knew the way we had come, across the Plain of Omalos. It stretched away before me, a plateau about five miles across in the middle of the mountains, and on the far side of it, a mountain village.

If I were to test myself, this was how I would do it. I would cross the plain on foot. I would move close to the Greek earth, yet surrounded by clear ground. I would put myself in the middle of that wide space where I would not be touched. I am not afraid of space.

The sun had dropped more than I realised when I set out, or

perhaps there was cloud descending on the mountains. It was much colder than it had been in the ravine. I told myself it was bracing.

I would not have seen the things I did that afternoon if I had not walked across the plain.

At ground level, and obscured by the dead winter foliage from the bus where we had passed before, I could see whole carpets of blue and red anemones. I took out my camera and aimed it in the general direction of the flowers. I felt ridiculous at first, thinking that the flowers would see how inept I was at using a camera, and then laughed at myself, at the silliness of shooting off picture after picture at such crazy angles and without consideration for the way the light fell. I had not used the camera before. It had been my father's and it had been insisted by my family that I carry a camera. I had not wanted to take it because I cannot take photographs. I have resisted learning because I am afraid I will not take the very best of photographs. Oh, that is quite true. That is how I am.

What I did not think of then, but do now, is that my father had used the camera to take pictures of flowers which he would later paint. Subtle little watercolours. He was old when he began to paint but even then, he was not bad. No, better than that, he was good, but he left it too late to be the best. I think he might have been if he had begun when he was young. That was his tragedy you see, to have failed at so many things, when he might have been the best at this one thing. The very best I mean. I do not exaggerate.

Anyway, that was what I photographed on my travels, that and nothing else. Flowers hidden under dead branches. Months have passed and I have still not had the film developed. Perhaps there will be nothing there. Maybe I won't have it developed.

On the flat fields, shepherds minded flocks of rangy sheep. And hundreds of people collected wild vegetables and herbs, tiny plants which emerge in the spring and have to be burrowed for in the earth. The vegetable gatherers sought the tiny *stawya-gathi*, each one no longer than a finger, yet they carried bulging sacks. As I passed, their glances would flick across me but their expressions changed little.

So I arrived at Omalos, a little after four, and sat outside the *taverna* to watch the people of the village. I watched discreetly and from a distance, I did not cast bold glances in their direction. They filled the centre of the village and it appeared as if a celebration was in progress. On the tables stood bowls of freesias and irises. Slanting-eyed girls were learning to flirt. I wondered how long this would last, for I had observed that women in Greece were grave and industrious and worked while their men sat in the sun and looked at women tourists.

A tractor hauled a trailer load of young men backwards and forwards through the village past the girls. The girls peeked and giggled.

At length, a man approached me, and offered food and a glass of *retsina*. He said that the food was special — it was a dish of something that looked like curious little batter pancakes with proved to be filled with a mixture of very strong herbs and a cheese-like substance. They were quite delicious. I accepted this food with modesty and downcast eyes, not looking at him — or not very much, although I did see that he had blue eyes, which in itself was exceptional. But I was careful, for I did not wish to antagonise the women. That care was to no avail.

The party folded, the air grew colder with mountain chill, and I moved inside the *taverna* which was run by a very strong-looking though quiet young woman. Many people came and went as the afternoon wore on and she entertained them, offered hospitality, but not one inch would she give to me. I asked for, and paid for food, I asked for the use of the toilets and she pretended not to understand me. I showed her my phrase book — '*Ghinekon, ghinekon parakalo.*' She tossed her head. 'Lavatory please, please your lavatory,' I said.

She pointed over her shoulder and looked the other way. If she looked at me at all that afternoon, her look was always cold.

The man came back with more food. I refused him. I smiled, but I sat very still, not accepting him at all by movement or gesture.

No one else spoke to me.

A young French couple, dressed as in the time of hippies, came in. They had hitched up from the town. They hired a room for the night above the *taverna* for three hundred drachmas. I asked them if they spoke English. A little, they said, and we talked but not for long. They had not come to talk to strangers, only to each other. The villagers welcomed them. I could see that it was because they were a man and a woman together, a couple. No matter how they looked or dressed, it was this togetherness that was understood.

The cold began to frighten me. This was deep biting mountain cold. My kidneys ached.

New Zealanders who fought in the war are buried in Crete.

They fought on the beaches alongside the Greek people. At school, a girl in my class was called Crete, and her little brother, Maleme. I asked the woman for a brandy and she told her son to fetch it for me. I said to her, '*Eema Naya Zeelandya.*' I am a New Zealander. A special kind of pleading. She appeared not to have heard me and I did not say it again.

Her legs were perfectly clad in dark stockings and she wore neat laceup shoes but her feet danced when she moved and she never missed her step no matter how much she was carrying from table to table. She continued this dancing unfaltering step as she walked away from me.

The bus came at last, sounding its high fluting horn as it crossed the plain which led to Omalos. The bus was full of vegetable pickers from the plain, and we descended from the mountains, moving into hairpin bends as if to pass over the edge of each cliff, and then as we came to the valleys the strong heavy scent of the orange groves came up to meet us, and the temperature rose again.

I ate, as I did every night, at one of the waterfront restaurants, surrounded by the hordes of tiny half crazed and mangy cats which hunt in packs on the Chania waterfront, and I waited for the scarlet sun to fall into the sea.

But I chose a different kind of restaurant that evening, one which sold bland Americanised food. I liked to eat Greek but my stomach was in rebellion. I asked for a half bottle of wine such as I had every evening on the waterfront, but this restaurant did not have half bottles, only a large carafe-shaped jar. For those who travelled alone, the choices were to be dry or drunk or out of pocket. As I was about to refuse the jar, a woman at the next table spoke to me.

She said she had bought one of the jars but she did not need all the wine either. She asked me to share it with her, and that was how I came to join her.

Her name was Anneliese, a Dutch woman with long straight iron grey hair and wide cheekbones. Her face was clean of make-up. She spoke flawed but elegant English, and she asked me if I minded her smoking roll your own cigarettes. I reminded her that I was her guest.

She too travelled alone.

The waiter brought two meals although she had already eaten and I had ordered only one. I said I would buy her the fresh dinner if she would help me drink the jar of wine. She said she was still hungry and, like me, she had come here because her stomach needed a rest from oil.

We ate and drank and sat by the lapping water and the night submerged us.

I told Anneliese about my children and her face grew sad.

She smoked awhile, then said: 'I would like to adopt a child.'

'Why can't you?' I asked.

'Because I am not married.'

'Can you not have a child?' I asked.

'I've thought about that, but I could not carry a child without love for the father. I could love a child for itself.'

'Have you never loved a man?'

'Oh yes,' she told me. 'For twelve years, and I thought he didn't want a child, and neither did he think so then. Then he went away, and he had a child whom he loves with a woman that he does not love. He wants to come back to me.' Her voice was full of tears, but she did not seem to be a self-pitying kind of person.

'Won't you take him back?'

'No. Because I cannot take him from his child.' She shook her head, as if in disbelief.

'It seems like a muddle,' I said. 'But yes,' I added hurriedly, for she looked at me as if I had not understood. 'I can see you're doing the right thing.'

'It's no good, soon I will be too old to have a child and too old for the authorities to allow me to adopt one. I would take any child, any child in the world that has nowhere to go. I would take a black child, a brown one, a sick one, if it had no parents. It doesn't have to be like me, I don't seek my own image.'

I said that in my country adoptive parents were not always held in high regard, that there was a backlash towards women who took other people's children, that it was regarded as a political act against natural mothers, to take and adopt their children. I said this with a trace of bitterness.

She regarded me intently. 'So there are no lonely or abandoned children in your country?' she marvelled.

We both smiled, relaxed from the wine, and a little lazy about following up absurdities, although not so much that we did not, mutually, remain inscrutable about our position in relation to the absurd.

'Are you a feminist?' she asked.

'I suppose so,' I said. 'Aren't you?'

'Well . . . I believe so. What else is there . . .?' She hesitated. 'It's hard to know what one is here.'

She had long cat-like eyes. I thought she was beautiful. She made me think of my friend in New Zealand who wrote to me care of each poste restante, good, vigorous, loving letters. And other friends. Those of us who touched, trusted, moved up to each other and away, protected and protested on each other's behalf, in our own ways. I thought of the dark Greek woman with dancing feet and of the blue-eyed man at Omalos. Had she been protecting someone? Was she like us, after all? But if that was so, why had she not seen me as I wanted her to? Why had she sat in judgment upon me, and why had I failed?

'What are you looking for in Greece?' I asked Anneliese.

'I don't know,' she said, as if startled. 'What are you?'

I shook my head. 'I'm not certain. I see things and they go away.'

It was true, and even now it comes back to me only in flashes of brightness, and a whiteness in the mountains. There is little to hold on to. I thought I would write to my friend that night and tell her about this, and about my day. Only days before she had said in a letter that she had come to the conclusion that it is moments lived most intensely that are often soon forgotten, or somehow erased. They leave their mark, she said, but the edges become blurred.

I did not write the letter and she will have to make do with this, after all. It is the nearest I can come — to holding on I suppose.

When I parted with Anneliese we looked searchingly at each other. I was going to give her an easy kiss on the cheek and I think that that was what she had in mind too, certainly I would have embraced her, if we had not, at the same moment, changed our minds and withdrawn from each other. I cannot be certain what she thought then, but I suppose she may have considered, as I did, that it was not as simple as that.

We shook hands, firmly and gravely, and looked at each other in order to remember, as best we could, what we saw. We walked separately into the Greek night on a Sunday that wasn't Easter.

At the Homestead Hotel

'We've been trying to get in somewhere decent all day,' the woman said at dinner. 'And look where we've ended up. Isn't this revolting?'

There were six plain tables in the dining room of the Homestead Hotel, each covered with light plastic cloths patterned with a lace design. The tables were placed close together so that everyone in the dining room heard what she said. Other guests turned to nod their agreement and they were all so near to each other that they could take up the conversation from where they were sitting. Some commented on the old floral carpet underfoot, others on the quality of the meal, which though ample was of the roast and three vegetables variety; still others mentioned the small stuffy bedrooms they had been allocated and the mosquitoes that infested them, especially in the annexe where the ceilings were so low that the men could hardly stand up straight in them. And the Lord only knew what other bugs might be lurking in the woodwork.

The woman's husband looked vaguely embarrassed and glanced at his watch as if he had somewhere to go.

'The view's nice. I wanted to come here,' said the young woman opposite them.

'Oh. The view, yes.' The woman who had spoken first turned her head and looked at the landscape, and turned back to her meal, her face set.

The young woman, whose name was Cassie, continued to gaze into the distance. It was full of a dazed gold light. A long paddock, more like a rolling plain, stretched away from the hotel to a far belt of gum trees. The grass bent and shimmered before a light breeze, and the colour of the grass expanse was a delicate reflective blue green, changing as it moved. The gum trees were the same and even the sky appeared green around their outline, except for their white trunks. Closer, the dining room opened out onto a wide old verandah which ran right around the hotel at ground level. The garden beyond that was flanked by thickets of bougainvillea and hibiscus, and planted here and there were dense unpruned citrus trees bearing late fruit which laid a sharp scent on the evening air. Cassie breathed deeply.

'That's what I said,' the man commented. 'I like the view. Why can't you make the most of it, Miriam?'

She said nothing, so that the man turned back to their companion and said, 'You can get too used to chrome and shag-pile motels, can't you? I mean, we've spent half the day waiting for the public relations people to ring around for us and missed out on a trip on the bay. Well, we could have been out sight-seeing on the boat, but we've missed everything now.'

'I think we should go home tomorrow,' said Miriam.

'Where do you come from?' Cassie asked her, making her voice light and pleasant.

'Auckland.' She turned back to her husband. 'I told you we shouldn't have come in February. All the people who've been waiting for the school holidays to finish come in February and it's just as bad as January. We should have waited till March.'

'I'm Alan Forbes, and this is the wife,' he said to Cassie.

'How d'you do.' Cassie smiled at them both, but already she knew that her presence would be of no help, for it was clear that Alan liked her appearance, and Miriam had noticed this too. Cassie imagined they were wealthy, but while Miriam might have practised having money for a long time, Alan was barely aware of what was expected of him. His shirt was open at the neck over a greying thicket of hair, a gold pendant nestled in the base of his throat. There was a coarseness about him, conveyed through thick hands with heavy hairs along the fingers, hands which looked as if they had done manual work once, before success had overtaken him.

The conversation was hurrying on in the way of holiday-makers seeking faces for their albums, or at least for his part it was, and Cassie always found conversation irresistible. But there was an edge of danger in this one, as if the slightly drawn woman in beautiful casual clothes might suddenly snap, or bite one of them. She had very nice teeth, much better than Cassie's own. Cassie thought she could probably bite well.

'You're a photographer, then?' said Alan. 'What are you pho-tographing?'

'Nothing special,' Cassie told him. 'Well, no, that's not quite true. I lived here when I was very young. But I'm on holiday now. I've always remembered the light here. I wanted to take pictures in this light. Of the light, in a way.'

'You're taking pictures of the light?' Miriam's voice was incredulous.

'Sort of. I know it sounds silly. Well it was something I wanted to try, and my mother offered to stay with the children.'

Miriam's eyes flicked over her. Cassie was round, a little overweight, with eyes like dark honey, and a bobbed brown fringe. 'You don't look old enough . . . you don't look older than my children,' Miriam said.

At the end of the verandah there was a courtesy bar. Guests were able to serve themselves and put the money in a drawer under the counter. When Alan and Miriam walked past the open door, later, Cassie was sitting alone, drinking brandy and smoking a small cigar. She looked moody and tired.

'Cheer up,' called Alan. 'Look at the view.'

She smiled faintly. 'It was a long trip today. I came up on the Road Services bus.'

Miriam had walked on ahead across the lawn, towards the car park.

He lingered. 'Come with us, we're going for a drive.'

'Where to?'

He named a bay. 'Miriam's got it into her head that she'd like to buy a beach place round here. I expect we'd have to build it though . . . I guess we wouldn't find a place she liked that someone else had built. Lucky I'm in the building business. Anyway we've heard there's some places out at this bay, and there's still land to be bought there too. I thought we ought to go tonight. Just in case we do go back tomorrow.' He shifted on his feet and looked over his shoulder, but Miriam was already sitting in the car, staring straight ahead.

'Won't she mind?' Cassie knew her voice carried complicity, but the bay was far beyond her walking range, and it was a place she wanted badly to visit.

'Of course not, love to have you along.' She knew he had regretted asking her straight away, but he was committed, and so in a sense was she.

The light does not cease in the north until late on summer evenings. The orchards are bound by hakea hedges which are a pale sharp green tipped with red, like a light flush of fire amongst the leaves. The banks cut away at the edge of the roads are red clay, the dust lingers above the metalled highways. In the Forbes's car the air was close.

'I can't breathe,' Miriam said once.

'Do you want to turn back?' he asked.

'Yes. No. Are we nearly there?'

'I don't know, how should I know that?'

'By the distance, didn't you take it? You're always talking about your tripmeter, as if it matters a damn except when you need it.'

But the bay was around the next corner. They came upon the settlement, a long line of houses built close to the shoreline. The sea was flat and glossy, like an ironed cloth, and the first lights being turned on in the houses were reflected on the water.

'I can't believe it,' breathed Cassie.

'You like it then?' said Alan.

'Yes. But it's more than that. I used to come here when I was a child. When you said you were coming here I couldn't believe it, that you'd actually drive here. I used to come on school picnics on a barge — you could only get in by boat then. You see,' she added, by way of an apology to Miriam, 'I really am older than you think.'

Miriam ignored her. 'I want to go for a walk on my own.'

The car had barely pulled up when she opened the door and leapt out. Her shoes were low heeled but still not suitable for the beach. She held her purse over her arm and her scarf blew up in her face as she reached the waterline.

'It's her age,' he said awkwardly.

'Should we go for a walk too?' asked Cassie, not wishing to watch her from this distance. She knew that if Miriam were to look back they would look rigid and disapproving, sitting one in front and one at the back of the car, as if waiting for her to return, but it would be worse if she were to go and sit in the front with him.

She slipped her shoes off so that she could walk barefooted through the sand. Her feet were small and shapely and her toenails were painted bright red. He brushed her arm once with his as they walked along the beach, and steadied her with his hand when she leaned down to dislodge a sharp shell that had wedged itself between her big toe and the next one.

'Are you married?'

'I told you, I've got two kids.'

'Yeah, sure. Doesn't mean anything these days.'

'Yup. I'm married.' She held up her left hand with its thick shiny band.

'Miriam didn't think you would be. . . . Your husband doesn't mind you coming away like this?'

'No, why should he?'

He shrugged. 'So you used to come here?'

Cassie stopped, and thought.

'Only once. Yes, I've been thinking about it. I only came here the one time. It was a most beautiful day. My parents came too. It was the school picnic, the big event. My parents were hard up you see, and we didn't go to many places. So I looked forward to this day. We took a lot of fruit and bacon and egg pies and tomatoes and orange cordial that had been made up, and a thermos of tea. It took, oh, an hour, maybe two, I forget now, sitting on a barge towed by one of Blackie's boats. Blackie, short for Blackwell you see, was a big man in these parts, he owned a lot of the boats in the district. When we got here we put out a rug on the ground like everyone else. I'm trying to remember where, but there were no houses here at all. Not one. There was a lot of white shell on the beach. A blazing white, so bright and hot you could hardly walk barefoot across it. The children changed into their bathing suits and before long we were all in the water. There was one boy in my class who was a lot bigger than me . . . that wasn't hard of course, I've never been very big . . . but I thought he was my friend, because I helped him with his reading. I was sent to do it by the teacher. But he can't have liked me at all, perhaps he really hated me, thought I was superior, how can one tell? Anyway, that day, he nearly drowned me. He came from under the water and pulled me down and held me. At first the sea seemed green and frilly beneath the surface and then it began to turn black. I struggled and fought. When I thought my head would explode, and that I would die, he let me go.

'What did your parents say? Do?'

'Nothing. They didn't see it happen. So I could have died.'

'Didn't you tell them?'

'No. Because it was their picnic too, you see.'

He was silent for a moment. 'I want . . .' he began, and stopped.

'Of course,' said Cassie. 'Of course you do. Shouldn't we see if Miriam is all right?'

They turned to make their way back up the beach.

'Cassie, I'm drowning.'

She reached out and touched his arm lightly. 'Perhaps. People drown every summer.'

'You should understand.'

'I'd like to do underwater photography,' she said. 'I'd forgotten until this very moment, telling you about it, that there was light shining through the water, the sun was actually bright even though I was surrounded by water.'

Miriam was standing outside a house close to the beach. The house was built of stained timber and it was long and low, moulded more into its surroundings than most of the neighbouring houses. Although it was new, it was like the Homestead Hotel in that it too had a wide verandah almost at ground level, with only glass to the floor dividing the interior from the landscape. This verandah was also festooned with bougainvillea, as well as passionfruit, and a tub of zinnias made a bold splash in a corner. Inside, a lamp had been lit, so that the room was plain for all to see. There were Persian rugs spread about, brass and pewter shone with a subdued gleam from the shelves of a splendid dresser, the light was soft on the coral-coloured walls. There was a large dark bowl of shaggy white daisies on a low table. A woman with thick grey hair piled up on her head was seated at a piano, with her back towards them. She was a large person, but when she turned her profile slightly towards them, the features though prominent, even hawk-like, were finely drawn. Cassie guessed she might be Turkish.

The woman at the piano paused for a moment from her playing as if she was unaware of their presence near them.

Miriam turned to Alan. 'That is the house I want,' she said in a low voice.

'I'll build it for you,' he said easily.

'No. I want that one.'

He took her arm and steered her along the beach, for the woman in the house had begun to get up from the piano. Cassie followed along behind them.

'I could come back tomorrow and ask her if it's for sale,' he said.

'It won't do any good,' said Miriam. 'That's hers. She won't sell it to you.'

'Then why say you want it? I don't understand.'

'It's the only house I want. How can you understand? It is the only house I'll ever want.'

They reached the car before Cassie, who had trailed further

55

behind them. She thought of not returning to the hotel with them, but the evening light, filtered through the trees, was falling towards them like a heavy green curtain, and they were half an hour's drive from the township. The road was quiet, as if few cars came this way except those of the residents and the day trippers. It was too nearly night. Cassie heard the word 'slut' as she approached the car, before Alan turned on the ignition to block out what Miriam was saying.

As Cassie started to get into the car Miriam opened her door and got halfway out, as if she too had been thinking of walking home. She hesitated, changed her mind. She appeared to have also considered the distance.

They would have driven back in silence if Cassie hadn't talked about her children, and started to describe her four-year-old son's tricks and turns of phrase, and soon Miriam began telling her of her own children when they were small. She said, then, that Cassie must take their photograph in the morning if she would, of course they would pay for the film, but it would be nice to have their photo taken by a proper photographer while they were on holiday, and they would take hers too, of course it would only be a snap but it was fun to remember the people you met when you were away.

The warm scented night had fallen completely on the hotel when they drew up. Cassie suggested that they should all go to the courtesy bar for a few drinks together. 'It's sort of quaint being your own barmaid,' she added.

'They must be very trusting here in the country,' Alan said, stalling for time so that Miriam could make his decision for both of them.

But, 'No,' his wife said, 'we've had a long day. Young things like you can keep going longer than us. Besides, I'm allergic to cigars.'

Later, as it drew towards midnight, Cassie was shuffling cards at the table beside the bar. The two barmen from the public bar next door had joined her and one had his girlfriend with him. They were the only ones in the hotel still at large. The four of them had had too much to drink. Cassie wished she had gone to bed. The mosquitoes were clotting the lightshade; she had a large bite swelling rapidly on her forearm. As she scratched it she glanced along the verandah, thinking she heard a footstep.

Alan had just stepped onto the lawn and was walking across

to the carpark, not looking in their direction, as if unaware that they were there. He reached his car and placed his arms on the roof, leaning his head in them for a moment. Then he appeared to look straight at them, although from that distance his face looked like a blank white hole. Across the space Cassie sensed the blankness of horror. A shiver of recognition passed through her. She sat very still and did not tell the others that they were being watched. Soon he straightened up, and turned to go back the way he had come, still not looking to either side of him.

'Drunk,' said Cassie. 'I'm drunk.' Nobody was listening. She clutched the edge of the table.

At the door of one of the annexe rooms, Miriam stood in her nightdress, the light out behind her but clearly visible in the moonlight. She watched Alan cross the lawn, going back to her.

Beyond the Wall

Jeremy Ordway is contemplating a wasps' nest that must be removed before Sunday when he hears Eunice Brown singing in the church, over the sound of the organ. There is a touch of supplication in her reedy voice. He knows she would like him to go into the church and talk to her and he is not entirely averse to the idea. But he will not; it is not appropriate, and he has work to do. Her voice falters on, *There is a green hill far away / Without a city wall / Where the dear Lord was crucified / Who died to save . . .* there is a crash of chords, a lid drops shut . . . *died to save us all,* quavers Eunice, and falls silent.

In fact there seems to be a great silence all around him. Though if he listens he knows he will hear things on the solemn autumn air. For things are never what they seem.

Straining, he hears the shimmering whistle of Dash McLeavey working his dogs in the far paddocks, and then his voice, *c'maway c'maway now halt there Rusty c'maway here here* and the sad isolated cry of a cornered sheep. And coming along the road towards town there is the rattle of the iridescent green Subaru ute owned by Mortlock Crane, who is his plumber, a sensuous-looking man with a full fleshy mouth for whom he has noticed his wife Sophie makes melting moments when he calls. Poor Sophie, he does not begrudge her her moments for Mortlock. Indeed, it has gone through his head more than once that some small advance by Mortlock, some reason why she could scream and clutch her breast and go to sleep dreaming might not be a bad thing.

Perhaps she would say yes. Yes, Mortlock, enfold me to your greasy heart, God will take care of us.

He raises his hand in salute to Mortlock, and his wave is returned. Mortlock will be eager to please. There is business in the air.

His eyes lift to the steep sides of the grey-tiled church roof, to the rusted guttering where a green and luscious line of grass grows along its edge.

And then it happens.

Crash. Crash. Slither. Tinkle and crash. Although there has been no perceptible movement of the air, only Mortlock's ute driving past, something has dislodged four more tiles from the roof.

They lie splintered at his feet.

As he stands contemplating them and grateful at least that they have missed his head, for his bald patch is covered only by a handkerchief knotted at the corners like a small tricorne, a voice calls merrily *hullo hullo, and how are we today*? Jeremy wonders if he can avoid looking around and knows that in decency, he cannot. It is Glen Frew from the Gospel Hall.

Glen saunters towards him, amiable and pleased with the world. When Jeremy sits on the church roof, which he does quite often these days, he can see clear across town to Glen's spanking new brick and decramastic hall (it is they who have deemed it a hall, he has decided, he makes no apology for refusing to call it a church) and he concedes that he is envious. What matter that he represents the church of the country, the true word? The state of Anglicanism must still be measured against Glen Frew's gospelling. His hall does not have tiles falling from its roof, it is not about to be invaded by the elements, it is proof against many things, wind and water, and yes, wasps too. It has no beams arching high and shining above the stained glass windows, ruby and turquoise and purple and gold like the cohorts of the Assyrians. But it is proof against the weather.

'A great old building, they don't build them like that any more,' says Glen, too heartily, looking at the church roof, which has begun more and more to resemble the gumminess of an old woman whose teeth are falling out.

A wind stirs in the branches of the acacia tree alongside them, all aglitter with silver light on the underside of its leaves. There is a promise of rain in the distance.

Any moment now, Jeremy thinks, he will offer me 'his boys' to come and mend the roof. He prepares a stiff response to indicate that the matter is under control, yet at the same time not giving away what he has in mind to remedy things.

But he is saved the trouble for another voice is calling him with an imperious urgent sound, and he thanks Sophie in his heart for being as she is, a woman who might melt momentarily for Mortlock, but will not tolerate her husband standing around gossiping with fundamentalists.

He gives a sigh of mock resignation and excuses himself from what Sophie describes as 'that dreadful Frew man' and walks across the shaggy lawn towards the vicarage. Inside the church

Eunice sings with renewed vigour *oh dearly dearly has he loved / and we must love him too . . . try his works to do.*

Sophie keeps the blinds in the sitting room drawn halfway so that the sun will not fade the Sanderson linen covers of the large armchairs. She sits in the dim light with a tragic air. The brass table that her uncle brought her from India gleams and scarlet dahlias in a cut-glass bowl cast a glow but she projects a delicate presence against them. Jeremy notes how quickly she has arranged herself among the cushions since her stentorian roar across the grass.

As he had entered the house he heard the blare of the transistor radio which Sophie always keeps beside her wherever she is in the house. But at his footfall it is snapped off.

He looks down at her and remembers how beautiful she has been. Still is perhaps, only now he notices the outline of food in her slender throat when she swallows, and the telltale yellow tinge of ageing in her teeth. But her hair is dark and curly still, only lightly tipped with grey, and her skin is magnolia-like, perfectly preserved and waxen in its purity, touched lightly with make-up. She is dressed in a correctly pleated linen dress with padded shoulders and drawn threadwork on the bodice. It is dusty pink. She extends a fine hand towards him. 'Where were you?'

'You know where I was. That dreadful Frew man caught up with me.'

She nods. He has struck the right note. 'Ah yes. Indeed. And what did he want?'

'To commiserate.'

She flashes him a look, a touch of cunning tinged with triumph.

'Four tiles,' he says. 'There have been four tiles down already this morning.'

'It will be all right,' she says.

'What was on the radio?' he asks, knowing that he must.

'Forrest Fleming. I wanted you to hear him. There's just been the most marvellous talkback. I could hardly pick it up, but I got it, very faintly. He was talking at the end of his last campaign. He's raised two hundred and thirty-five thousand dollars for St Dorothy's in Justville.'

'Well,' he says. Then he says it again. 'Well.'

For what else can he say? He is impressed.

'There must be a catch,' he says. 'It sounds too good to be true. Such a small town.' He is thinking of the huddle of houses across the flat plain that divides his parish from the next.

'It is smaller than ours,' says Sophie with triumph. 'It will be all right, we will save the church, I know. He'll save it for us. Oh Jeremy, I know you don't like the idea of a professional fund-raiser to find the money for the repairs, but it's the only thing. You do see, don't you?'

There is something touchingly girlish about the way she clasps her hands. Her fine dark eyes flash with excitement. How can he help but love her for her enthusiasm? And a bishop's daughter as well. How envied he had been when she had said that she would marry him. How the cathedral choir had sung.

'There,' he says, 'I've already agreed, you don't have to convince me.'

'We should tell Eunice,' she says. 'It was her idea. To be fair,' she adds, as a subtle way of reminding him that although the organist has had an inspiration, only she, Sophie, had the foresight and the drive to carry it through. Or the contacts. 'Eunice is in the church, isn't she?'

'Ah yes,' he says. 'The wings of song. Practising away in there. Couldn't you hear her?'

'A tiny sparrow,' says Sophie, in sudden poetic flight. 'I heard the notes squeezing — squeezing up.'

'Through the holes in the roof.'

'Oh Jeremy, what is the matter? Why don't you believe? What's happened to your faith?'

When he does not reply she says, 'If you are going near the church would you tell Eunice that I am about to heat some pumpkin soup?'

As he recrosses the lawn Jeremy sings under his breath. To the tune of 'There is a Green Hill' he whispers *What is the matter oh by gosh? / What is the matter — oh? / What is the matter — er — er?* When he enters the vestry door he raises his voice, giving a sign to Eunice that she commence playing again. But the other woman in his life has already packed up her papers and the organ lid is down and locked. She has heard him but she pretends that she has not.

Instead she kneels at the altar rails in a prayerful attitude. Her slight frame is clad in a scrubbed yellow sweatshirt and a brown dirndl-like skirt that flows around her bent form. He sees her roman sandals peeping out from underneath and winces.

In spite of her signal to keep his distance he approaches Eunice Brown, local organist, dressmaker and cub mistress. He is, after all, her spiritual mentor. Well, isn't he?

'So what *is* the matter?' he asks.

Eunice gives an exaggerated start, which he decides to ignore. He sits on the altar chair and fixes her with what he hopes is a penetrating gaze.

'Oh why can't everyone be happy?' she cries, seeing that he is unmoved by prayer.

'My dear Eunice,' he says, 'I am delirious with joy. Why should I not be?'

'You are not,' she says. 'Forrest Fleming is coming to save us, and you're going round with a face like a fiddle.'

'He may be coming to save you, but I may be beyond Mr Fleming's redemption.'

'How can you say that?' She bends her head, suddenly ashamed. 'Oh Father Jeremy,' she says, 'forgive me, it is only He who saves us I know. But the church. Mr Fleming is His instrument. Surely we must have faith in something or everything will fall down around our ears.'

Jeremy is unconscionably moved by the sight of her scrawny neck bowed before him. He has never touched Eunice Brown's neck but he senses that it may be softer than it appears.

He looks up towards the roof. He could swear he can see light shining through.

'Did you hear the story about the church out in the bush? It had a light above it. No? Well they put the power lines through, this was way back, you know, and the electricity was a miracle. So. To the glory of God and the power supply, the locals put a neon sign over the church. Proclaimed the house of the Lord for all to see. One night the church burnt down, so what did they save?'

'The sign?' whispers Eunice.

'Of course, Eunice, the sign. Well there you are. Churches come, they go, but old Claude Neon, he keeps on getting his cut. You can't be too careful.'

'That sounds like the way they used to sell television sets and refrigerators to people before they got the power put in,' she reflects, entering into the spirit of the story. 'Well, something like that.'

'It does, doesn't it?' he says in a hearty amiable way.

She reacts as if stung, tries not to blink the unshed tears which threaten to roll down her hairy earnest face. 'You made that story up, didn't you?'

He is silent for a moment, and still. This is the house of the Lord, which, in spite of everything, he loves. And he is not without affection for Eunice Brown.

'I heard something like it once,' he says after while. 'It is a story not entirely without truth.'

And because she is Eunice Brown she believes him. Why should she not? It is a kind of truth.

When they have eaten pumpkin soup and wholemeal bread washed down with squeezed lemon juice (it keeps them healthy, Sophie says), Jeremy retreats to the garden to consider anew the problem of the wasps' nest. He must also think about Sunday's sermon, for with the arrival of the fund-raiser there is a real hope abroad that the church will be at least half full.

But he has barely set foot outside when he hears the telltale slide of more tiles broken loose and skidding down the roof of the church. Around the bell tower a large gaping hole has opened up.

Above, the sky is full of rushing and accumulating clouds and beyond the edge of the town the paddocks lie blue and jade, shadowed by the onset of the approaching rain.

Sophie has relented and made tea. 'You've been practising so hard for Sunday's service,' she says to Eunice.

'Yes. Yes, I have.'

'I'm sure it'll be lovely.'

'I'll do my very best.'

'But of course you will. You're not nervous, dear? No, of course not. There, will you pour the tea?'

'It's just that he sounds such a remarkable young man . . . Sophie, there is no tea in the pot.'

'Oh my dear, how silly of me, there it is in the china pot. You see, I polished all the silver today.'

'Of course. I should have thought.'

'I polished it ever so hard. Look how bright it is.'

'It's beautiful. You keep things so nicely, Sophie.'

'La, old habits. Look, I can see you, Eunice, reflected in the teapot. What a strange shape you have. Coo-ee. You've got a big head. And little arms. Ooh. Now, you've got bosoms.'

'Don't.' Eunice's voice is sharp, and suddenly wary.

'Oh dear, you're cross. My little joke. Why not be light-hearted? I've worked hard for his coming too, you know.'

'It's hot,' says Eunice, 'it's so hot.' She walks to the window, stands looking out. She sees Jeremy but does not signal to him. She savours the moment of watching him, unaware that he is being observed. 'But it may rain before night.'

Behind her the phone shrills. She hears Sophie pick it up, but her end of the conversation passes over her.

When Sophie has replaced the receiver she calls in a frightened peremptory way to Eunice. 'It was him, Forrest Fleming. He is calling here this evening. He has asked to stay the night.'

'But he is not due until the weekend.'

'He wants to start planning the campaign straight away, he says he can't wait to begin now that he has finished in Justville. He'll be here in a few hours.'

'Oh Sophie. Will you manage all right?'

'Of course. Of course I will. I must breathe deeply. I must think of father.'

'Indeed.'

'But you must help me Eunice.'

'And so must you,' she tells Jeremy when she has summoned him. 'I'll give you a list to take to the shops.'

'I haven't got time,' he says. 'The hole's got bigger. I have to get the ladder up.'

'You must,' she repeats impatiently, as if he is a child. 'Did you not hear what I said? You don't have to worry any more. He's coming tonight.'

'Tonight? Our friend Mr. Fleming will fix the hole in the church roof tonight?'

'Well not exactly. But it's the beginning.'

'If we get a real storm and it gets under the tiles . . . there won't be any church left to save. I have to do something.'

He runs up and down, distractedly plucking a raincoat from its peg on the hall door and banging in the kitchen cupboard where he keeps a hammer and some nails.

'You can't go up there now.'

'I need some pieces of wood to block up the holes.'

'I'll go to the shops,' says Eunice.

'But I need a whole ham,' says Sophie. 'Now that things are underway. Who knows, I may need to cut sandwiches. Well, you can't carry a ham in your bike basket.'

'I'll get some slices, and the rest can be delivered tomorrow,' says Eunice.

The rain has still not come; the cicadas still sing; the air presses close upon them. The feverish sound of wood being sawn assails the air, a harsh scratch and rasp, and something else, what might be taken as an oath if one did not know that this was the house belonging to a man of the cloth.

Jeremy has cut his finger and it is bound with a flapping length of bandage that he has rushed in and seized from the first-aid kit in the bathroom. He saws backwards and forwards at the wood but he is getting nowhere.

Sophie moans quietly to herself as she concocts a pastry. She knows that the best puff pastry should be rolled seven hundred and thirty times on a marble slab and takes at least a day to prepare but there is no time for that. Thanks to Julia Child she acknowledges that in an emergency *feuilletage rapide* will suffice though even that takes time and its toll.

'We should ring Dash McLeavey, he could help.' Eunice has returned from the shops, and stands transfixed at the windows. An ugly wind is stirring; it suddenly whips the marigolds backwards and forwards, catches Jeremy's trousers and tugs them against his knees.

Sophie lifts haggard eyes towards her, and shakes her head.

In the garden, Jeremy thinks, will I or will I not ask Dash McLeavey to help me. As he swipes through the wood again with his bent and buckling saw, attempting to quadrate some forms that will match the roof tiles, he has a vision of Dash's thin face, a face so toughened by the weather as to suggest that he is a man without feeling. Yet it is Dash who has comforted him when, kneeling before Jeremy he has said in agony, dear Lord, why me, upon the death of a son, and Jeremy, considering himself a man without concept of the death of children, though he has been called upon often to confront the subject, has said, I do not know, Dash, I do not know.

There is a splash of rain on his face and the air chills. But then the rain stops.

'He doesn't think I understand anything,' Sophie says.

'What does he want you to understand?'

Sophie turns the pastry again and sighs without answering. There is still naked butter gleaming against the pastry's fold.

'I'll go,' says Eunice abruptly. 'I'm poor company.'

'No don't,' cries Sophie, as if suddenly afraid to be left by herself. 'Look, this campaign was all your idea. I'm not really much use, you know. I polish silver and arrange flowers, prepare food. I'm not a person of ideas,' she admits.

She does not say, although it is clear what is on her mind, that without Eunice's support Jeremy cannot be relied upon to continue with the campaign, or show sufficient enthusiasm to Forrest Fleming to convince him that it is worth his while.

'I pray, Eunice,' says Sophie. 'You know I do pray.'

'I cannot imagine what he will be like,' says Eunice, speaking of Forrest Fleming. 'I feel such a sinner.'

At this Sophie laughs. 'You a sinner? Oh no.'

'It's true. I need to confess.'

'Oh not that again.' It is a source of private embarrassment to Sophie, particularly when she recalls her upbringing, that Jeremy has so embraced the reformation. Sometimes she secretly genuflects when she goes into the church. It pleases her when some of their parishioners call him Father, as Eunice sometimes does. But Jeremy is determinedly and utterly Low in his approach to ecclesiastical matters. He does not believe in confession. She sometimes wonders why he is Church of England at all when the options are so clearly laid out.

Still, she says to Eunice, when she has recovered herself, 'I'm sure you don't need to confess, dear, but if you're troubled you can always talk to Jeremy.'

'Oh no.' Eunice's face flushes. 'No, I couldn't do that.'

'Why, what have you done? Tell me. No one tells me anything.'

'I'm sorry.'

In the garden there is silence. Eunice strains to see what has happened to Jeremy but he has disappeared from view.

'What are you sorry for? Have you sinned with my Jeremy?' She gives another chirping little hiccup of a laugh. 'Oh that's good.'

'I'm sorry no one tells you anything.'

Sophie's pastry is done. She wraps it in a cold cloth and puts it in the fridge.

'Yes,' she says, when the pastry is away. 'Yes, so am I. President of the Mother's Union. Do they tell me when the Smiths' baby is sick? No, *she* has no children. President of the Wives' Group. Do they tell me when Harry runs off with Mary? No fear, I won't know what it's like. And the bishop's daughter and all. A good day when he met me, Eunice. They said it was ambition, you know, but Jeremy's not ambitious. It'll be easy, he said, you know the drill, and nobody needs to teach you how to pray. So I listen. I listen and watch all around me. And hear nothing, see nothing. I turn on the radio, the television. Blood, death, pollution, riots, war. I pray God to stop them, but what are they really, Eunice. What do they mean? No one tells me.'

Eunice speaks in a choked voice. 'It is a small price to pay for a pure heart.'

'Tell me.' Sophie comes around the kitchen table wiping her hands on the enveloping blue apron she is wearing, and takes Eunice by the arm, shaking her a little. 'How did you sin?'

'Pride. Vanity.'

'You? Oh I don't believe that. I'm vain. Jeremy says I am. Look, how do I look, I say to him. Smooth? You like my hips, my skin, is my colour good? Vain, he says. Well, it is something to know one has sinned. It is worth knowing that one deserves forgiveness.'

But Eunice has stopped listening to her. 'After that last dress I made for Mrs Moreland, I went down to the city. Remember that time?'

'Oh yes, I remember now. What did you do?'

'First I went into a hotel.'

'A hotel?' Suddenly this game has gone far enough. The weight of what Sophie is about to hear oppresses her.

'I felt a little faint. The crowd, you know. I had a little brandy. Well, I needed some courage.'

Sophie holds the edge of the table.

Eunice is inexorable. 'I went into a shop and bought a set of underwear. A brassière.'

'Uh, a brassière. You said a brassière?'

Eunice nods.

'You are rather slight, but goodness everyone, well I would have thought. My dear Eunice, that is no sin.'

'It was black lace, they were all black lace. French. They cost me a month's rent. You see? When there are so many in need.'

But if Sophie does see she cannot express herself except in hysterical laughter. She bends over the table wheezing and crying with laughter, Oh uh huh huh, she weeps, wiping her eyes and smudging her face with flour.

Then she stops as if she had never begun. 'Jeremy,' she says, and looks at him standing in the doorway.

Eunice swings around. 'You heard?' she says to him.

'Yes,' he says. 'I heard.'

'It is funny, really it is,' Sophie remarks, as if to convince them all.

Eunice has gone very pale. 'Listen,' she says urgently to Jeremy, 'afterwards I was ashamed. I put them in the mission box. For the blacks, you know. To cover their nakedness.'

'It is so funny, isn't it, Jeremy?' says Sophie.

'No. It is not.'

When Jeremy has gone, Eunice turns to Sophie. 'Don't you know why no one ever tells you things?'

'Where are you going? Don't leave me,' wails Sophie, but it is too late.

At the door Eunice relents a little. 'Oh I'll come back. And so will he. Don't we always? But I cannot bear it in here. I cannot bear it.'

They are all gone, and Sophie is alone. She begins to clean the kitchen with systematic care. She has a sauce to make. Then she is shaken with laughter again, but this time of the silent helpless variety. She recalls the black lace underwear she has discovered in the mission box. The set sits tastefully packed in tissue in her own bottom drawer. It is funnier than they think.

There is a chord of thunder. The sky is electric with lightning. Jeremy struggles with the ladder against the wall.

'Mr Ordway, Father Jeremy, what are you doing?' cries Eunice. She tugs after him as he ascends the ladder, and succeeds only in untying his shoelace.

He puts his hand tentatively over the guttering and pulls himself up level with the eaves. Everything holds. The rain has started in earnest.

'You'll slip,' calls Eunice.

'Be a good woman, dear Eunice, and go and collect some hymn books from inside,' he replies as he swings his leg up onto the roof. He reaches hand over hand, inching towards the bell tower. When she stares back, without moving, he calls out impatiently. 'Nine tiles today, you see, and four yesterday, two the day before. Fifteen, I need fifteen hymn books.'

Now Eunice sees the abandoned pile of wood that he has been trying to saw, barely scratched from his exertions, and understands.

'To fill the holes? You can't.'

'Don't worry. They know it without the books. A green hill, without a city wall. Soon there will be a church without a roof. We must shore up the breaches. And hurry, the storm's breaking.'

Soon she is at the bottom of the ladder with an armful of books. He inches back across the roof, and comes halfway back down the ladder. 'No, you must not try to climb up, here hand them to me, good, very good Eunice. Now . . . if you'd be kind enough to . . . hold the ladder. Splendid.'

'Are you all right?'

'Ye-es. But things are getting a trifle slippery. Could you sit on the end of the ladder my dear while I climb up? Good, yes that is good.'

'Shall I come up too?'

'Good grief no, what should I tell the parishioners on Sunday if I had dropped their organist through the roof?'

'I'll wait for you to come down.'

'No, it won't take long. Go and keep the peace with my wife. And don't tell her I'm up here. All right?'

'All right.'

'They fit perfectly, I am mending the roof beautifully. Now go on out of the rain.'

He sings in his light baritone worn smooth by years of intonation. The wind is lifting small objects on the ground, last spring's fallen birds' nests, and papers brought too late for the church drive, a gust of confetti from a recent wedding, and an armful of Michaelmas daisies which he has cut back in his search for the wasps' nest. There is something exhilarating about being up here alone against the elements.

'There you are, God,' he remarks loudly, 'that's quite a nice job. Aren't you pleased with that?' For the hymn books are such a snug fit in the holes where the tiles have been that it is as if they had been made for the purpose of mending roofs alone. But at that moment a howl of wind whips across the sky, nearly knocking him from his feet.

He grabs at the bell tower and his foot skids. Suddenly it is a long way to the ground, and his feet do not seem to be connecting with the roof as well as they were. Gingerly, and still holding onto the slats supporting the bell tower, he sits down.

'Lord God,' he says, 'I am very nervous about being up here. I am not as good at being up on high as I imagined. I've done a good job, and I want to get down. Now don't scare me. Please.'

But God throws cold water in his face.

'You are not helping,' he says. 'I wonder sometimes if you and I are incompatible. Quite often think that. How, for instance, does one both defend the faith and pray for deliverance from wars? You see, I don't make the rules, dear Lord, you must forgive those of us who sometimes find it difficult to stick to them.'

His voice is torn away in the lashing gale that has risen around him. The hood of his oilskin is snatched from his face, exposing it to the rain. He begins again in what he hopes is a reasonable tone. 'I know you're not up *above*, or out *there*. But you're around somewhere. I know. My good wife Sophie has told me so.'

'Dear Lord, I provide a lot of things. Inspiration for polished silver, black brassières for the mission box, and I'm sorry that I have not seen to the window in the church hall. Now will you please let me get down from here, because I have been filling the holes in the roof of your church. And I have become afraid. Now if I move a little . . .'

There is a crack, familiar now, but closer at hand. Tiles tipple across the roof, so many he cannot count them as they skate over the edge. Nor can he afford to look, for now his left leg hangs down the hole that has been left in the roof, swinging backwards and forwards above an exposed beam within, and his fingertips clasp the iron strut above.

'We're thrilled to meet you, Mr Fleming,' says Sophie. 'What a miracle your last campaign has been.'

He smoothes his hair with his hand. Forrest Fleming is not at all as either Sophie or Eunice have foreseen. Although neither have voiced their expectations, both know that in each other's imagination they would have looked for him in a dark suit and a tie; perhaps a touch of suaveness. Instead, he is dressed in canvas drill slacks and a cream open-necked shirt that reveals a tuft of delicate gold hair at the base of his throat. He wears thick-lensed stylishly rimmed glasses on the bridge of his prominent nose and his casual grace suggests a cross between an intellectual and a wind-surfer. When he smiles he reveals even teeth with a gold filling in the front.

'I'm not sure about miracles,' he says. 'Good business, I suppose.'

'And prayer, surely?' says Sophie.

He gestures delicately, gives a deprecatory half-smile.

'Well, there you have me,' he says.

Sophie shoots him a look, comprehends, straightens her back. 'We must find Jeremy,' she says. 'Do you know where he is, Eunice?'

But Eunice has just looked out the window again. She raises her knuckles to her mouth.

The strut has begun to bite into Jeremy's flesh. It has drawn blood. Water streams through the hole where his leg is trapped; he sees the puddles collecting under the roof, sliding through the lining, knows it is running down inside the church. He closes his eyes as if to allay his mental picture of the sullied altar linen beneath him. Though it makes better viewing than his own predicament.

Soon, soon he must let go. But, he thinks, maybe that is the way things have been heading for a while.

'Hold on,' calls a voice. 'We'll have you down in a tick.'

He opens his eyes and sees Forrest Fleming coming towards him across the roof, agile as a young fast-footed antelope. Tiles crumble and fall.

'Bring more hymn books,' Jeremy calls in what he hopes is a jolly tone.

'What?'

'Oh never mind.'

His hand is prised from the strut by the capable young man, and a rope is lashed around his waist.

'The miracle man,' says Jeremy as they inch across the roof. 'So it is true.'

Dinner is a success; Sophie glows in the light of compliments. They scoop *bleu de Bresse* out of its slatted wooden tub and scoff it with unceremonious gusto at the conclusion of the meal; they have drunk three bottles of Mission wine (what fun the monks must have, remarks Jeremy), replenish their coffee cups, become excited, their eyes shine with story telling.

Only Eunice falls quiet. 'You won't be in church on Sunday then?' she says, turning to Forrest Fleming.

'Oh, if you would like me to be, that's fine,' he says.

'It's part of the job?' says Eunice, with an edge.

Forrest leans across the table. 'It is a matter of percentages,' he says. 'What is yours, Miss Brown?'

She colours. 'A Christian tithe,' she says. •

'Ten percent of all you earn?' he says mercilessly.

She winds her napkin around her fingers.

'The campaign was Eunice's idea,' says Jeremy hastily. 'She is a more than generous giver.'

'I will raise my donation,' Eunice says, faltering.

'No, that's impossible,' cries Jeremy, who knows that Eunice's ten percent is derived from an income gleaned in painstaking stitching for farmers' wives who have more money than she, from alterations, and mending gym slips, from bridal gowns such as she has never worn, from ballet dresses for precocious children, and from fancy dress costumes for ungrateful debutantes whose mothers cheat her. And he sees her bending towards the sheet music above the organ each Sunday, pretending she does not need new glasses.

Forrest smiles understandingly, but there is something melancholy in the way he looks at Jeremy. Turning back to Eunice, he says, 'That is over to you, Miss Brown.'

'I have brought some vodka,' says Forrest, when he and Jeremy are alone by the fire. Outside, the storm has abated, the pounding wind died amongst the acacia, and the rain turned to a gentle patter on the vicarage roof. Sophie has run Eunice home, despite her protestations that she will cycle. I have a light; I have a coat, she has said, but nobody has listened to her. That is her fate, thinks Jeremy.

'Sometimes at the end of a long day,' says Forrest, explaining the vodka. 'Well, not everyone is as generous a host as you.'

And, 'Why not?' cries Jeremy. 'Let's have a vodka. Or two, if your bottle's large enough.'

Which it is.

'Can I ask you something?' Jeremy is into his third.

'Try me.'

'Would I be able to do your job?'

'*You?*'

'Ah, I thought not.'

'You'd take things to heart,' says Forrest Fleming at last.

Jeremy leans forward, staring into the flames. 'You cannot know,' he says, 'how I have dreamed of some other life. Of going beyond the wall. At first, it seemed to me that I should be a man like my friend Dash McLeavey (now there's a man who will give us money), noble and natural. Or a man like Mortlock Crane, who will give us no money but may be prevailed upon to do the spouting for a discount on a Saturday morning, and makes women happy; but then, when I began to think about it, I thought that I should like to strike out on some other more original life of my own. For a long time I thought that I should like to be a lift attendant in a tall building, deciding how high and how low people should go, in the real and physical sense, listening to conversations that were not intended for my ears, instead of the careful curse-free ones that are prepared in my presence. Or a butcher. That shocks you? Cutting up dead creatures for people to eat? Oh well, it is just that I should like finding the grain of the meat, discovering the secret pleasure of taste. And slicing salami. I could pretend I was an Italian. How I have always admired Mediterraneans. It is to do with their architecture, I suppose. What marvellous churches. Well, I am none of these things. How do you see me, Forrest? Tell me truthfully. Don't be afraid.'

When Forrest Fleming answers, his voice is so low that Jeremy strains to hear him.

'A shadow boxer,' he says.

Jeremy nods his head backwards and forwards, sighs.

'Yes,' he says. 'I suppose that's true.'

'With tenacity in the clinches.'

'You think so? It is worth holding on?' He leans forward, grasps the vodka bottle by the neck and tips it towards his glass. He holds it out to Forrest.

'I am glad there are miracle men,' he says. 'And I'm not into takeovers. No.'

He smiles, pokes the fire; the log hisses. Tomorrow he and Eunice Brown will scrub the sodden altar carpet, and his wife Sophie will wash the stained cloth.

The Courting of Nora

She watches Harry from out of the kitchen window and knows when he is still halfway up the paddock that there is something wrong, and without being told, or even running through a list of possibilities in her mind, that the horse must be sick. It is hardly a surprise, for through the winter there have been many days when it seemed as if the old creature would never make it onto her feet. Sometimes they would have to coax her with pieces of sugar and other blandishments. But once she was up, the mare would set off without faltering for the house, and the window of the room where Nora's father lay. Then it seemed she might live forever.

This morning it is different, and when Harry walks in there is an edge of panic in his voice, as if the order of things is about to be changed; though they have expected and in a secret unspoken way, more than a little hoped for this, the reality is alarming.

When he spells it out to Nora she sits down at the table. The remains of their early breakfast is still strewn in front of her, along with yesterday's *Herald*, the accounts she cannot put off paying any longer, and her father's tray bearing a cup of tea, smoky with the skin of milk on it, and the remains of some thin porridge spread with melted butter and honey swimming on a plate.

She puts her reading glasses on, then takes them off again and rubs her eyes.

'I thought she'd be better in the spring,' says Nora at last. 'Won't she budge?'

He shakes his head. 'You'll call the vet?' It is both question and answer.

'You're sure it's that bad?'

For the farm is too small in these days to call an economic unit. They have to watch every cent. Harry once said to her that she might do all right if she changed to goats, that was the coming thing. Either that or bring in more land from the back, and put in new plant. By she, he had really meant them, but it has not been possible for them to make decisions together about the farm, or to think about moving away from cows. Harry has built up the pig side of it, but he could only do that because the

74

old man had had pigs before the accident. There'll be no new-fangled ideas round here, he'd said.

The pigs have helped but still there's no spare cash. Nora's hand-knitted cardigans have leather patches on the elbows like a man's, and the ute breaks down often on the way to town, so that the neighbours in their new Japanese cars have to stop and give her a tow or send someone out from the garage to help her. She thinks that they must laugh to themselves, the way the old man used to carry on in the past, as if he were worth a fortune, and here they are now about the same as the alternative lifestyle people with eccentric houses up the valley, barely subsistence farmers.

'I reckon you better get the vet,' Harry says.

They have talked about what they will do when the time comes, but it has always been difficult to imagine it exactly as it will happen.

No, that's not quite true, for she has seen it one way or another in her mind's eye a hundred times, and the variations are so small you could hardly pick between them. The scenario, as they call it on television, is that Harry would walk in one morning and tell her that Trixie is ill, and that they must get the vet if they are to save her life. Then she will tell her father, lying sick in his room, that the horse is not coming to the window that morning. Her mind always stops at this point, although sometimes she dreams of the outcome. It is a tortuous dream that leads her through many byways, but when she has woken from a dream like this, she has been panting, or even weeping guilty tears, and sometimes her body has been covered with sweat, and there is a damp painful ache where her hand is resting between her thighs — although that hasn't happened now for a very long time. Years maybe, but in the light of day she does not allow herself to think about it and so she cannot be sure.

Well, so far the first part has happened the way she has seen it, the strange part is seeing it unfold like that. It's just like television, like one of the shows where you know what's going to happen, but can't quite believe that they'd do anything so predictable, only then they do. So television is like real life after all.

When she rings the vet clinic she is told that no one is going out their way today, unless it's urgent. Of course that will cost more, though the girl on the other end doesn't say so, in fact she doesn't sound as if she cares much. Nora says that yes, it is urgent, the vet must come at once, or sooner, the matter is of the greatest possible urgency, it is the horse Trixie, as if she would know immediately that someone must come, but the girl continues unruffled, barely remembering Nora, which is not surprising given how long it is since her last call. She agrees at last to send someone.

Nora looks at the door of her father's room. There is no sound behind it. He will sleep for another half-hour, then wake on time, as if to clockwork, to await the arrival of Trixie.

She clears the dishes from the table, quick and methodical now, half expecting the vet to materialise at the gate in moments, though it could be hours before he comes. Perhaps she is panicking too. She breathes deeply and evenly, willing herself to move steadily and sensibly through the day and to do each thing that has to be done in its proper order. The top of the heavy old table is cleared now and shines in the light through the windows. She has washed the flowered curtains the week before and the linoleum, though worn, is like a hospital floor, not a speck of dust anywhere, and that isn't bad for a farmhouse ninety years old with timber that snaps and shrinks at the seams on frosty nights. She has cleaned things, year after year, as if in preparation for something she cannot, or will not name. Nora finds she is listening to her own breathing, and walks out to the garden to listen to the movement of the grass instead.

Spring has unwrapped the buds on the plum tree, the river shines in the distance, the morning lies like golden wine about her, and the cat rubs itself against her legs. Ah so sensual, her breasts pain her, and there is a tugging at the base of her belly, a drawing down, so that she knows her period will come before the week is out. She is still alive, her body still functions. Her hands flutter to her tender breasts and she lets them rest there a moment feeling the nipples rise. It is so long since that has happened too, more often her breasts feel like scones. Her face reddens, shy and surprised. She glances around quickly but the empty paddocks stretch away before her. The cat rubs its bellyful of kittens against her legs. 'This is disgusting,' she says in a loud firm voice, and straightens her back, so that it twinges too, to remind her of her body's impending condition.

The moment cannot be delayed any longer. The half hour has been a reprieve, but the time is passing, might already be up. Sure enough, her father's voice flutters from the bed when she opens the door. His fingers are clenched round the edge of the blankets and his eyes stare at her with violence in their depths.

'Where've you been?'

'In the garden. It's such a nice morning.' She sees there is a white scum round the sucked-in corners of his mouth and that it is beginning to bubble into a froth.

'Where is she?'

Nora moves to straighten the covers on the bed but his hand shoots forth and grabs her wrist so hard she cries out. She knows the power in those scrawny fingers and usually she is better at avoiding them. She thinks, if she moved away forcibly enough, that her greater strength and weight would bear him along bodily behind her out of the bed, but that he would not release his hold.

'Tell me, Nora, tell me.' Despite his anger, and his grip on her, his voice is pitiful. He farts loudly and having begun to pass wind he is unable to stop, his body racked with spasms. A foul smell envelops them.

'We've sent for the vet,' she says faintly.

'Have you seen her?'

'No. I was waiting for you to wake.'

'Go on down. She'll come for you.' He is quavering.

As she walks down the paddock she thinks that that will be the nearest her father ever comes to paying her a compliment.

But his faith is misplaced. Harry sits with the horse but it does not move. Only the tender pucker of the mouth and the erratic fluctuation of the faded roan flanks beneath the blanket are evidence that she is still alive.

'How's he taken it?' Harry asks Nora when she kneels beside him.

'Reckon he'll go clean off his head.' She talks to the horse, wheedling and prodding, producing sugar and a new carrot from her pocket. It is no use. Harry watches and listens and adds words of encouragement, and Nora wonders why, why are we doing this, what will become of us? For fifteen years this horse has visited her father's window, every day since he was scooped up in one dreadful movement by the baler from the field of hay. The animal is long past its time to die, for it was not a young horse even at the time of the accident. Yet in living on, it has given the old man something to look forward to each day, it has in its turn kept him alive.

But why that, Nora wonders now. Why Trixie the horse, when there could have been so much else that he's denied them, and could have shared with them. She is thinking of children she might have had. Come to think of it, now she doesn't know why they let him do it. There seemed to be reasons once, but it was all too long ago, and now they don't make sense any more. It is simply that the passing of the years has whittled their resistance away until there is nothing left but this rundown farm, and them. Her and Harry. Two odd people inhabiting a patch of land that neither can lay claim to, and no longer have the courage to leave.

She looks at Harry with his furrowed face and grizzled hair. When first she knew him it had lain in tight little curls all over his head, now they start halfway back on his head, and instead of copperiness they are an indeterminate brown streaked with grey; the bony forehead starts out more prominently over the deepset eyes, the funnels of reddish hair that cover his body jut out under the too short cuffs of his working shirt.

That is what she sees, and as the vet comes towards them across the paddock she tries to see what she must look like to him — a tall, too thin, ageing woman, a little stooped, with fair cropped hair, hands that look like Harry's, wearing a crumpled khaki overall, clean, note that, but crumpled, looks as if she's never used an iron in her life, and a cardigan with patches . . . all right, Young and Handsome, so what are you going to do about our horse?

'Why don't you go back to the house?' says Harry. 'I'll take care of things here.' He will too, that's Harry's role, taking care of things. Of her? Maybe. Maybe that's what he does.

The vet is even younger than he first appeared. He is new to the local practice. She supposes he knows what he is doing and leaves him in consultation with Harry.

Back at the house she enters the room with stealth. The old man pretends to be dozing but he doesn't fool her. From the smell she knows she will have to change the bed and supposes that's why he pretends. He is at her mercy. Indeed, his life has been in her hands every day for all the years he has lain here. Yet for all that, he is the one who has stayed on top, he is the boss. Only today he wants information. If, as he usually does, he makes out it is her fault for leaving him that he has messed himself, then she might withhold what he wants to know. Not that she would, surely dear God he knows that too, just goes to show how it matters, that he should even briefly fear her power.

A photograph of her mother in a heavy gilt frame stands on the dressing room table, and one of her brother alongside of it, the boy who should have had the farm but got himself killed instead. The men in the family haven't had much luck. As she regards the two faces, carefully composed for the camera, she catches her own dishevelled reflection in the mirror. Have any of them had luck? Faded blonde, the vet might say if he was describing her to anyone. Not original, but it fitted. Pleats under the chin, and pale today, oh God yes, but she was tired, so what about her bodily functions, just let them be over soon, they get in the way and don't make a scrap of difference to anyone.

'Put your shoulders back, Nora Duthie.' Her father has stopped feigning sleep. 'Nobody'll ever dance with you,' he says.

'When has anyone ever danced with me?' she answers, without turning.

'Never mind, you'll get a decent fella yet.'

'Shut up, damn you.'

His barbs are not without point, of course. They always are. By the time she met Harry she'd stopped going to dances. Chaps didn't like a woman who towered over them, and when she stopped that didn't seem to do much good either. Harry was the hired man. He never got past sitting in front of the fire with her in the evenings and listening to the hit parades on Saturday night. Hits. My God, now that was a long time ago. Long surpassed by television. She was taller than Harry too, but as they didn't dance what the hell. Hell. Yes, hell. All of it was hell.

From the bed the old man starts to sing in a reedy whispering voice: 'I wish I were in Dixie, hooray, hooray . . .'

She goes to him and he clutches at her hand, but not so that he will hurt her this time. Tears squeeze out of the corner of his eyes. Playing for sympathy.

'I'm sorry, Dadda,' she says, giving him the old childish name. She hasn't said it in years. If she hadn't said that she might have said, die, you old bastard, hurry up and get it over.

Out in the kitchen there are voices, Harry's and the vet's.

'I'll come and fix you in a minute, all right?'

The young vet's face is full of regret. 'There's really nothing else for it. She'll have to be destroyed,' he is saying.

Nora closes the door firmly behind her as she joins them. 'You can't do that.'

'The animal's in pain. I can't leave her suffering.'

She shakes her head, no.

'I've just been explaining to your husband . . .'

It's Harry's turn to shake his head. 'It's for Miss Duthie to decide.'

The vet looks startled but it's not his business to comment on their domestic arrangements.

So Nora tries to explain, in halting sentences, how the horse comes to the window every morning to see her father and that that is what keeps him alive, it is all he has. And this morning he is fretting already.

'Shouldn't you get the doctor then?'

'It's the horse he wants, not the doctor,' says Nora, and the vet looks at her curiously as if the thin greyish woman might be simple. Still, she goes to the phone and rings the doctor, who is already on his rounds up their way, and before long the kitchen seems full of them all.

'I can't leave that horse to suffer,' says the vet as matter-of-factly as he can, when the doctor has given old man Duthie a sedative. 'The animal should be destroyed.'

Doctor Elliot is almost as old as the vet is young. 'And I can't allow you to destroy my patient.'

'I'm not God,' the vet says sharply and too loudly. He falls silent as they all look at him. He and the doctor consider each other awhile and the doctor is perhaps thinking that the vet is a fortunate young man to have learned such a complex lesson already.

'Will he really die? If the horse does?'

'How can I tell you that?' asks Dr Elliot. He is a round old man, overfond of the bottle and food. Harry often says he has seen him in the pub on Friday afternoons. It is Friday that Harry goes to the stock and station, and has a jug at the hotel. 'I seen Dr Elliot,' he says when he comes home, 'full as the family po again.' But the doctor is wise in the ways of his patients who are also his friends. He reflects now. 'It could happen, though. What do you think, Nora?'

She sighs and rests her head on the beam by the stove where she is turning pikelets for their lunch. 'I don't know. I don't think he knows how to die. Or you'd think he'd have done it by now, wouldn't you?'

Their silence thickens. 'I think he'll die though.' She ladles out more of the creamy mixture onto the stove.

The doctor says, 'I could have your father taken to hospital in the ambulance while he's sedated. We could try and keep him alive.'

You ought to do that. Something's got to be done,' says the vet, wishing to end the dilemma.

'Oh so that's your advice, is it?' snaps the doctor, thinking that the vet hasn't learned much after all. But maybe it's not his fault.

He looks at Nora and then at Harry. He has known one of them a lifetime, and Harry — well, long enough. Nora places food on the table as he watches them; the steaming pikelets, a dish of tomatoes ripe from their vines, and some pale glossy ham that Harry has cured. She uses a *Reader's Digest* for a mat under the fresh pot of tea. The rough hands shake, she is not used to so much company. On her left hand there is a thin worn ring which has become part of her, as most women's wedding rings do. Only this isn't a wedding ring, but a small insignificant engagement ring; it wasn't expensive when Harry bought it for her all those years ago, the year of the accident.

The idea of Nora marrying the hired man who came in for the haymaking hadn't pleased her father. Since the accident with the baler he had had fifteen years of lying under the coloured coverlet that Nora's mother had made out of patchworks and scraps of bleached flourbag to think about it. It pleased him even less after all this time than it did at the beginning, which he was fond of telling them. What it amounted to was this, that she could have the farm one day, but so long as he lived it was his, he was having no hired man marrying her with aspirations to a fortune, and his brother's sons would be pleased to have the place if she didn't behave herself. The fellow could stay for the milking, which he supposed being a woman she couldn't manage on her own, and that was all. No funny business.

If they'd gone just a few days earlier, in the full path of his rage, instead of staying around to finish the hay that fateful season, hoping that in doing so they would bring him round to their way of seeing things, it might all have been different, he might have gone to hospital and stayed there, or the accident might never have happened, or any of the other human variations that could be imagined might have occurred. Might. It didn't matter any more, none at all, his lying there year after year had made it impossible to run away. For Nora anyway, and so, it seemed, for Harry too.

Even if she was no dancing partner, she had energy and a way of getting on with the work which suited him, who'd been after his own place for a while, and worked here and there, sometimes on the roads, sometimes on the farms, a man from nowhere special. Perhaps it was true, that once he had sought a fortune, although looking at the Duthies' place he must have decided to settle for rather less. He'd stayed around one Christmas and bought her perfume from the Rawleigh's man. She'd told him to go away once or twice and then she'd let him stay.

Now the ring with its diamond chips is dull and plain like its wearer.

'His time's got to come,' the doctor says. 'Shall we just wait and see what happens?'

She jerks her shoulders up and her eyes burn. 'You've no right.'

Dr Elliot looks back at her. 'I've done as much as I can. Haven't you?' He spreads raspberry jam on a pikelet with delicacy, skimming the knife. 'There's a time, you know.'

He eats the pikelet and takes another one. In a reflective way, he says, 'The hospitals are full. It's not usual to admit a man because his horse is dying, you know.'

In the afternoon the horse dies, and the vet who has felt oddly compelled to stay comes to tell her before leaving to make up his lost day.

In the night Nora and Harry take turns at watching beside the old man's bed. He opens his eyes once and whispers in singsong, 'I wish I were in . . .' and lapses back into a sleep or a coma.

'Soon, soon,' says Nora, and while her back is turned, fetching Harry, he slides off the edge into death.

In the morning when he has been taken away, the bed turned down and the windows opened wide, Harry comes up from the milking, and from burying Trixie with the help of neighbours who have called since the word spread, soon after dawn. The room is quiet and empty except for the two of them, a hiatus in the comings and goings.

'The Hammonds say you can board with them if you like,' says Nora. 'I can hire you for the milking if you want to keep it on for the moment.'

'The Hammonds?'

'You can't stay here. It wouldn't be right.'

'And us?'

She slides the worn ring off her finger, dislodging it with difficulty over the knuckle. 'I'm not sure that I'd know how to be married now, Harry. Not to . . . well, change anything, you understand.'

He nods. Nobody watching her would know whether she was disappointed that he hasn't argued with her, or whether it is what she really wants. It is unlikely that she knows herself.

And there is no time to think about it for the arrangements have to be made and lawyers to be seen (the old man has been meticulous about his affairs, the lawyers had their instructions to attend at the house once every six months, for the old man was never sure that Nora wouldn't try to take over the farm behind his back; they had told him she couldn't but he didn't believe them and each time they called they had to produce his will for him to check each page to make sure it hadn't been tampered with), there is the decision whether to have the organist or not (she decides she will) and whether to have the funeral the next day or hold it over three days because the gravedigger will be away (she decides on the next day) and in no time at all it seems, since the horse took sick, on a sour day to which winter has temporarily returned, they are burying Nora's father.

The service is brief. Afterwards the cortège winds its way into the hills to a small hillside cemetery where Nora's mother and brother and grandparents lie. Only a few cars follow the hearse into the hills, for Duthie was never a popular man in the district and no one knows Nora well enough to feel more than a passing compassion, and even then they are not quite sure what form their sympathy should take. Or that is what their eyes say as they look uneasily around the tiny gathering, only its smallness reassuring them that it was a neighbourly thing to come. The old man's brother, Nora's uncle, leans on his stick and watches his two sons and Dick Hammond, Harry, and two other neighbours who have stood in as pallbearers carry the coffin to the grave. It is the presence of the other dead that reassures Nora, standing in the brisk wind, dressed in a cream crimpolene dress revived from the back of her wardrobe for the occasion. She has thought of touching up the outfit with a scarf of her mother's, kept away in a drawer, but it is green streaked with vivid red, and at the church door she decides that it is unsuitable after all. Instead, she moves quietly to the edge of the grave and lets the scarf fall amongst the sullen clay. The neighbours look at each other and away, and afterwards one of them is heard to say that there might be more to Nora Duthie than meets the eye, and perhaps they have not thought well enough of her in the past. But what they think is not known to Nora, which is not to say that she does not consider the matter. That is why Harry is being sent to live with the Hammonds.

He moves forward awkwardly to stand beside her. He sees her as tall and fair and very beautiful but he cannot quite reach her to kiss her cheek. He touches her hand instead. The congregation averts its eyes again.

'Nora?' he murmurs.

The voice of my beloved spake . . . Nora feels his touch, hears him. Her head is full of biblical response. After all, it is a solemn occasion.

'Y'all right then, Nora?'

'I'm okay.'

There is a scurry of rain and they gather themselves for a dash to the cars. She catches her foot and nearly trips on her grandmother's grave. Three generations of Duthies, almost a family cemetery. That'll be it, she thinks, except for her cousins and their families. They don't feel like blood but she supposes she has to count them in. And at least she has her bit of a farm. She feels she has wrested it from them and doesn't much care. Her grandfather cut his land in two and gave half to each of his two sons — they were supposed to farm it together, but her uncle had sold up, so hard luck, uncle.

But it is hers now. The land and the old tumbledown square-cut farmhouse. All hers.

And empty.

So goddamn empty, as the spring passes on into summer. The cat splits open with her kittens like a fat yellow melon (she is a ginger cat) and for once Nora doesn't drown them. Correction. It is Harry who has drowned kittens for her before. Now that he's not here she can't do it herself. And the cat is so pleased and the kittens are company. Also, her father is not here to smell them. He always could, even from his room, and above his own stink. Now she can do what she likes.

She doesn't see Harry often, or not to talk to, though they talk business at the shed some mornings. The first week that he is gone she writes him a note at the Hammonds' place suggesting a timetable for the milking and offering him one day a week off for as long as he chooses to keep the arrangement, and a month's pay in advance. She offers to help out at the shed too, although with the herd as small as theirs he has done most of the milking on his own in the last few years. He drops her a note back, stiff and very formal in his out-of-practice hand, saying that he can manage all right, though he'll accept her offer of a day off.

The days that she milks are harder than she expects and she is always tired the next day. It is difficult to accept how much she had come to depend on him.

But the weather stays kind and she slips into a routine that more or less suits her. Some nights she watches television too late and when she stands quickly after she has been sitting for hours she may be dizzy for an instant, but apart from that she is well. She wonders some evenings if she should ring Harry and check that he is satisfied with his terms of employment. Or if he will stay when the cows go dry. That is something she would rather not think about. She doesn't know where she would get someone else next season. Someone who would, perhaps, have to live in the house with her. That's something she doesn't think she could stand. She's only used to Harry. When she thinks that she turns the television up and blots out thinking.

By day she is too busy to think. As the summer proceeds she considers cutting down the number of pigs she runs. They are more than she can manage. One day she remembers the goats. A neighbour had Angoras, she's seen them when she's been driving into town. At the petrol station she mentions them to the woman attendant, who tells her that the goats she has seen are kept for their fleece. It's a nice idea, but not quite the same as a milking herd, which she had been contemplating. Though how nice it would be to sit and spin soft yarn.

Another day she is out staking the sunflowers. The kittens roll and bite at her ankles. Three of the five kittens are ginger like their mother, like small sunflowers themselves, plump, yellow and everywhere. A prolific time. She feels a slight ache in the small of her back and suddenly it occurs to her that she hasn't menstruated for nearly two months. Slowly she straightens up, and the bright sunny day has a cool dark tunnel in it directly in front of her eyes.

She shrugs. It is nothing. Shock. Change. Harder work than usual. But deep inside she knows that the greatest shock is that it hasn't come. The ache in her back is reassuring, though. It means it won't be long and soon she'll be back to normal.

Only nothing happens. Or not to her. The plums ripen and fall from the tree. This year she leaves them bruised and rotting on the ground, and her body is unchanged. And nothing happens as the season turns and the hay is ready. So this is growing old, she says to herself, full of curious sad wonder.

She makes a point of seeing Harry at the shed. He has bought himself a small ute, and she has a slight pang when she first sees it, realising that he must have savings of his own, that he had prepared for an independent life while he still lived with her. Or perhaps it had been for them both, when they were free? But she has sent him away and now she cannot ask. Strictly speaking, she supposes she owes him something more from the farm, after fifteen years on it. But what? The first businesslike moves had seemed rational and sensible enough, now she is confused as to what she should do. She mentions the haymaking to him in a tentative way.

'It's fixed,' he says.

'What do you mean, fixed?'

'We always had the Rowse gang come in. They asked me the other day.'

'Asked you?'

He looks at her sideways. 'I'm sorry,' he says after a while. 'If you'd rather get someone else I'll tell them.'

'No, of course not. Who would I get? They've always been fine. It's just . . .' She turns away.

'They'll come next week,' he says, and gets on with the cleaning out.

That evening she picks a bowl of raspberries, cool and slightly sour, and sits on the verandah eating them with cream. The night draws in and she sees what looks like a flying saucer in the pale dark but it is an aeroplane far above, the reflection of its lights caught on a wisp of cloud. She has never been on an aeroplane and wonders what it would be like. Perhaps she will sell the farm and go away on aeroplanes? She does not know where she would go.

The night before the grass is to be cut for hay, Nora goes down late, after Harry has finished the milking, to see that all is well for the morning. Or that is what she tells herself, for there is nothing to be done, except that which Harry has undertaken already. The main paddock lies by the river bank and tall trees grow at its edge. In the morning the machines will sweep through, leaving the grass rank upon stubble and smelling as sharp as cider. Often when she was younger she had lain on the riverbank the night before the haymaking to get the last sweet scent of the grass before it fell. But it has been fifteen years now since she did that and the last time had been the first that she wasn't on her own, when she had had a lover to share the grass and the river and the evening with her. The night before the accident.

She drops onto her knees and falls forward into the grass, lies there. At first she feels foolish and pulls the grey cardigan tightly about her even though the evening is still and warm. But the earth is familiar beneath her and her body fits where she lies.

'I thought I'd find you here,' he says above her and she knows that it can only be Harry, though her arms muffle her ears. She starts scrambling to her feet but he pushes her back to the ground. A small scream rises in her throat and her eyes widen with fear.

'. . . to tell you, don't struggle, I won't hurt you, don't run away from me . . .'

She understands then that he means her no harm, although the thought may have passed through his mind, but more from anger than lust.

They sit apart and she is afraid he will go away without saying what is on his mind.

She cannot contain her curiosity any longer. 'What did you come to tell me?'

He turns the grass beneath his hand, this way and that. 'Well. If you aren't in too great a hurry, I could perhaps learn to be a married man.'

He waits and she says nothing. She thinks of the aeroplane that flew over the farm last week. There are so many alternatives, so many things that one might do, if you only knew how to go about it.

'You could think about it anyway,' he says. He takes the old worn ring out of his pocket and holds it in the palm of his hand. Nora reaches out and touches it, to feel its shape for the last time. He digs a little hole between the blades of grass.

'I'll help you,' she says, and they scrabble together at the soil. They bury the ring in the cool earth knowing that tomorrow the place will be covered over and impossible for them to find.

The Prize Ring

For weeks Peter Dixon had been wondering what his son Stephen would think of him when they met. Other times he would think that this was nonsense. Stephen was the one who should be wondering what his father would think of him.

After all, if Bethany's letter was to be believed, it was Stephen who was initiating the meeting. Peter was not at all certain that he even wanted to see his son. Their two meetings in the last seven years had been unsuccessful in a quite spectacular way.

But there it was on the page — Stephen has come such a long way. He and I really enjoy each other's company nowadays. His marks at school have been so good that I think I can almost count on him getting Bursary.

Bursary. And there had been a time when she didn't hold out much hope of keeping the spotty loudmouthed brute in the schoolroom after his fifteenth birthday. It was amazing. Then, the letter progressed, I'm not promising wonders at prizegiving, even though he's worked hard, I shouldn't think he is in line for anything major, but he has wanted to see you for some time now, and it occurred to me that this would be the last chance you had to see him in his school environment. Why don't you come over and see us? I realise it's a busy time of year for you in December, but we wouldn't expect you to stay long and, knowing you, Pete, I guess you can always wangle a bit of business in as well. How about it?

How about it? He had turned the question over a dozen times in his mind since the morning in spring when the letter came. Even now, standing in his hotel room and adjusting his tie and arranging his handkerchief in the top pocket of his suit, he could see himself standing on Alton Wharf waiting for the ferry and staring down into the water, trying to discover in its depths some answer to the difficult question of whether or not he should cancel three days' appointments in order to go rushing off to New Zealand to his son's prizegiving ceremony. Prizegiving. That in itself conjured up an archaic other world-liness that he kept telling himself he had left behind long ago. Since his second divorce he had shifted to Mosman, leaving his ex-wife Patsy and their son Jason in the apartment at Rose Bay. Natalie, the woman he was living with, said that she thought it was a silly idea, that the woman in New Zealand was so far in the past that he should leave well alone. It was bad enough having Patsy on the phone every other day wanting something or other, especially now she had a boyfriend of her own. Natalie was a dress designer and was planning to work at home for the day.

He was irritated by the fact that he couldn't have some room to himself to think about the letter, and resolved to put it out of his mind until he was cruising over the bridge, with a tape in the deck, just shifting along with the tide of the traffic. Then she had said wasn't he going to hurry if he was going to catch the ferry and he remembered her car was in the garage and that she had especially asked for the loan of his because she was going to see important clients in the afternoon. So that he was late, and missed the eight-thirty ferry and had to wait and he was fraught with anxiety because he had his first appointment at nine-thirty and he made a religion of never being late. It was crazy not to have taken a cab, but it was such a splendid morning that it had seemed extravagant. There was a time when nothing seemed too great an extravagance if that was what you wanted, but Patsy had made him rethink his finances a little lately. Natalie's tastes weren't cheap either.

As he leaned on the rail of the wharf, that seemed to answer it, in effect. He really couldn't afford the trip. Jellyfish like sucking white parachutes descended en masse in the water towards the golden seaweed at the edge of the seabed. Ah, that was him, getting sucked down and down by all these women and children.

For the last thing in Bethany's letter had been: You once offered to help me with Stephen. I've always felt proud of being independent and not asking for anything even in the sense of moral support. Looking back, I wonder if I haven't been a bit selfish in that respect, for it may have helped Stephen through some of his bad times if I had been a bit more forthcoming. But, right or wrong, now that we are through it and things have come right, I wonder if I could ask for something — it is financial, but it would mean more than just the money, it would be a boost to Stephen's confidence to know that you were prepared to help, so it is moral too, if you like. He would like to go to university (surprise, surprise, Peter, our son, maybe we weren't so dumb after all) but even with a bursary it will be very hard for him living away from home. Holiday jobs are hard to get and I don't think he will be able to save enough to support himself properly, at least in the first year. I think he should go, and my pride really does seem misplaced if I can't ask his father for something as important as this.

Sucked, he decided, as the ferry scuttled across the harbour towards them, and saw in the seaweed the gloss of Bethany's lovely hair.

And saw his hands shake ever so slightly now, as he looked at his reflection in the wall-to-wall glass of his bathroom in the hotel, and prepared to leave for Bethany's place. He tried to visualise Stephen as Bethany described him now and wished that she had sent an up-to-date photograph. If he had progressed so far, it was unlikely that he would look as he had two and a half years ago, with long greasy hair and an earring and filthy unkempt clothes. But though it was Stephen he was consciously trying to conjure up, it was Bethany, his mother, Peter's one-time wife, who kept swimming into view. Silly to have come. The last time he had seen her she had churned him up, created a horde of ridiculous and ill-considered fantasies in his head, made him feel inadequate and lovesick at once, both quite inappropriate emotions. He and Bethany were over and done with their lives together so long ago. Since he had seen her last, he had worked harder than ever before, been appointed to the board of directors, made new friends, finally discarded his second marriage, given up smoking and increased his physical fitness, got rid of the hint of a paunch that had been bothering him and made love to some of the most beautiful women in town. Most people had even forgotten that he was a New Zealander these days. Things were perfect with Natalie too. She ordered his house for him, organised the cleaners, called in the caterers, was discreet about their shared lives and looked like a dream. She was as ambitious to succeed in her own right as Patsy had been determined to do nothing. And by this December evening even his bank balance had begun to look up again.

Yes, Bethany really was a voice from the past, no doubt about that. So why did he think about her so often?

He manoeuvred the rental car into the driveway, wondering at its narrowness. It occurred to him that he could have made the concrete wider when he laid it but that the extra bags of cement had been beyond his means then. For a moment, when he opened the car door, he wanted to lean down and pat the driveway. His concrete. But he was afraid she might be watching from the window. Besides, he was looking down at the spot where he had scratched the children's names in the wet cement, Stephen and Ritchie. Oh God, that he should go in with tears in his eyes. Ritchie, dead so long now. The one who might have been like him. He would have been nineteen. The bridge of Peter's nose hurt as he pinched his nostrils inwards to stem the visible signs of his sorrow.

Another car was parked in front of him on the driveway, a large handsome car, and he wondered briefly if it could be hers, but saw a smaller car slightly less battered than her last one, but still old and showing incipient signs of rust, parked ahead under the carpark. He hoped she didn't have visitors.

When she opened the door he knew that in this he was to be disappointed, for behind her there was a light swell of voices. But it was still her, bright-eyed, the chestnut hair crisply streaked now with a band of iron grey and her wonderful breasts even fuller and slung lower than the last time he had seen her. A handsome middle-aged woman. When would he ever get over the surprise of her, each time he saw her again?

'You've come at last,' she said, and leaned forward lightly kissing him on the cheek, an open unabashed gesture, more relaxed and friendly than she had been in her greetings since their parting all those years ago. Because she was not alone he handed her the gifts he brought more awkwardly than he might.

'Roses, Pete. Oh they're delicious, what lovely tight buds. And — what is this . . . oh. Oh Peter, you shouldn't.' Their eyes met and slid away from each other. He had stopped on an impulse at a record shop near the centre of town, and though he hadn't the faintest idea what he was going to buy when he entered, as soon as he had seen the old Nat King Cole tapes done up under new labels and packed inside a long slim packet he had known that it was the right gift. How they had listened to the old seducer, night after night, as the records spun unevenly round on their battered turntable.

'You have got a stereo? . . . I can change them.'

'Yes, mod cons now.' She looked at them again and the long packet they were packed in. 'I thought they were chocolate almonds.'

'Chocolate *almonds*. Nat King *Cole*.'

She laughed, raising her face to him. 'You'd better meet my guests.'

A man and woman were sitting in the chairs on either side of the fireplace. The man stood up immediately; Peter could see how tall he was. He had thick, well-cut grey hair and his hands were delicate. His wife was dumpy and looked older than any of them, although she was dressed and made up with care. Peter guessed that she probably wasn't as old as she appeared and, even before any of them had spoken, that if she was Bethany's friend she was probably also an envious one.

'Matt and Jill Hawkins, Peter Dixon,' said Bethany.

Matt shook hands. 'Drink?' he offered, waving to an array of bottles, when they had exchanged greetings.

Peter flinched. 'I think . . .' He glanced at Bethany.

Matt laughed, an easy comfortable laugh. 'Silly, isn't it,' he said. 'Jill and I see such a lot of Bethany, you'll have to forgive me for not remembering that you used to live here.'

'Not at all,' said Peter. 'I'm pleased Bethany has constant friends. Scotch thanks. No ice . . .'

'And just a drop of water,' Bethany finished for him. Everyone laughed. Peter too.

'I didn't know you'd be so handsome,' said Jill with what he interpreted as coyness.

'You mean Bethany didn't tell you?' He glanced sideways to see what effect this would have on Bethany, whether she would blush or make a rejoinder. She did neither, merely picked up Jill's glass and handed it to Matt. Peter noticed that neither of them had asked Jill whether she wanted a drink. Matt poured a stiff measure of gin for his wife.

'Shouldn't we be getting along soon?' asked Peter.

'Five minutes,' Bethany agreed.

'Isn't Stephen here?'

'No, I thought he'd be back, but he's with Anthony . . . Matt and Jill's son, they're best friends, you see.' It was by way of explaining everything, the Hawkinses' presence, Stephen's absence, the lateness of their departure. 'And Abbie's staying over with Molly, that's their daughter, they're friends too.' The family permutations seemed endless. He felt a pang of regret that Abigail, the child Bethany had borne after their separation, would not be with them. Although she was not his, she looked like Bethany and in that had always seemed familiar flesh, a kind of kinship.

'He knows I'm coming?'

'Yes,' she said and he could see she was a trifle distracted.

'Should you ring them?' she said, appealing to Matt.

'They'll be all right. You know what it's like on break-up night, parties all over the place.'

Peter did not know what it was like.

'Anthony's their third, you see,' said Bethany, again for his benefit, as if she was redrawing a map in which he might discover his own location. Did he imagine it, or was her voice tinged with a small edge of wonder that he knew so little?

'Perhaps a quick call? Just to make sure they're on their way?' Bethany said.

Matt dialled and waited. The phone rang for a long time at the other end and he was on the point of hanging up when it was answered. He spoke briefly, lightly to the person at the other end, his son Anthony.

When he hung up there was a mild and barely detectable frown on his face which Peter might have missed if he were not a businessman.

'Everything's fine,' said Matt. 'They're going to meet us there. Do you want to come with us, Bethany?'

'I thought Bethany might like to come with me,' said Peter, stirring himself. 'If you'd like to . . . or would it embarrass Stephen?'

'Of course not,' she said. 'I was going to take my own car actually, but, well why not? Actually I think he'd like it.'

'Oh it'd be lovely for him,' said Jill, her voice tripping a little. 'So nice, his parents appearing *together* after all these years.' She looked awkward then, and as if she wished she hadn't spoken.

In the car Peter said, 'They seem like a nice couple. What's his line?'

'Matt? Oh, he's a jeweller.'

'Figures. I thought he could have been a dentist.'

'Why?'

'His hands. Very nice.'

'You don't miss much.' She twisted a large turquoise ring set in heavy silver on her right hand. He hadn't seen it before. Something stirred dangerously in him and settled again before he had time to dwell on it. They had arrived at the school gates.

'Will he wait outside, do you think?'

'I doubt it, you know how it is when they're with their mates.'

'No I don't know what it's like,' he said more sharply than he had intended. She looked wounded. 'I'm sorry. You and your friends seem so certain that I'll know how things are, but I don't. And to tell the truth, I'm nervous about seeing Stephen. The last time wasn't much of a success, was it?'

'I know. It was awful. But it'll be different, you'll see. I wouldn't have asked you if I thought it was going to be like the last time.'

'I thought Abbie might have come with us.'

'They were only allowed two guests each. The assembly hall's not really large enough for these functions now that the seventh form's so big.'

He was humbled that he had been chosen and said no more as he parked the car. His hands were sweating on the wheel and it took two attempts to edge the car into the position he had managed to locate. For the school grounds were full, and parents and pupils in their green and black uniforms were pouring towards the assembly hall doors.

If you counted the day of their son's funeral, he and Bethany had met each other publicly in the town only twice since their parting. This would be the first time in the whole fourteen years that they had made a formal appearance together. Again he glanced at her profile and his heart lifted. He was going with a beautiful woman to their son's prizegiving ceremony. They were two mature independent people who could choose to do this. They would go with pride. They had come a long way together.

They were handed a programme at the door and hustled up the middle of the hall to two seats on the central aisle. There was a buzz in the air, a muted ongoing excitement. On the dais was a table on which stood ranks of cups. Was there, by any small chance, the possibility that one of them might be for Stephen? Now that he was here, he realised how much he wanted one of them to be for his son.

The orchestra was tuning up, fine whining and twanging emerging from their instruments. A man in front of him turned round and said, 'Hullo, Peter, nice to see you,' as if he had been away for a short holiday. Peter raised an eyebrow to Bethany after he had responded. 'Gone but not quite forgotten, who was he?' he whispered.

'Ssh, Dick Webb from the newspaper office.'

'Of course. Yes. Should I talk to him some more?'

'If you want to. You don't have to ask me.' She looked amused, turned and peered around behind her.

'Can you see Stephen?'

'No. I was looking to see if Matt and Jill had got a seat. I expect they would.'

'Matt looks like a guy who can take care of himself.'

She said nothing; a teacher decked out in his annual prize-giving gown was calling for silence at the front of the hall.

A hush settled over the assembled pupils and parents. Some-where behind them a large fart erupted. A snigger swept through the crowd. Next there was a hiccup. Peter felt like giggling too.

'Some poor kid's got nerves,' he muttered.

Bethany shushed him again. The teacher at the front looked annoyed and peered coldly out over the assembly before announcing that the processional was about to begin.

The orchestra struck up 'Gaudeamus' and the staff and distin-guished guests, as the programme listed them, started streaming past them towards the dais.

Peter found himself pealing away with them, feeling as if he was bursting with joy . . . Gaudeamus igitur . . . you can echo zoo-oo moon . . . or that's what it sounded like, he never had known what the words were exactly, and it didn't matter, he couldn't see to read them in the programme but he was singing his heart out anyway, for his son, for Stephen who was cleverer than they thought and who was going to make it, in spite of everything.

But Bethany was glancing behind her again, and this time there was a startled horrified look on her face. 'What is it?' he said against the music.

'Nothing. Well, I just saw Stephen, that's all.' She tried to turn away but his eyes followed the point she had been watching and he saw his son's face. It swam before him, better-looking by far than when he had last seen him and he had grown taller, his hair was tamed and gleaming under the lights. But he seemed to be leaning forward heavily onto the seat in front of him and his face was flushed.

'Is he ill?'

'I . . . I don't know.'

The music had finished, the staff and guests were settled and the principal rose to speak. A voice shouted an obscenity and then there was another hiccup. Heads swivelled towards the source of the noise. It was Stephen.

One of the masters rose from the platform and strode quickly down the steps again. There was a sharp altercation, a short scuffle and then it was over. The principal began speaking again. Peter couldn't look behind him for several minutes. When he did, Stephen's seat was empty. Bethany's face was silvered with tears. She sat very still and made no move to wipe them away or draw attention to herself. In a few minutes her nose started to drip and Peter gave her his handkerchief, trying not to disturb the air around them. She took it without looking at him and drew it across her face. Throughout the rest of the long ceremony she clutched it, her knuckles white and unrelenting. The students came and went to collect their prizes. People clapped. There was a strange little hiatus when the hockey stick for the school's best player was presented. The principal said in a strained voice that it was for Stephen Dixon, who was absent, and passed on hurriedly to the next prize, but not before a gale of giggles had passed round the hall again.

Once Peter half rose, thinking to leave, but Bethany touched his arm, restraining him. It seemed like a long way to have come to witness (if that was what you could call it for he had not had the courage to look) his drunk son being carted out of his school prizegiving. Matt and Jill's son Anthony was awarded the proxime accessit prize. 'It means runner-up to the dux' Bethany whispered through the applause, moving from her rigid position of self-control. Peter couldn't have cared less. Then she added with a fierce bitter note, 'Anthony holds his drink better. It isn't fair. It's him that starts it too.'

A blonde girl accepted the dux's award as if she had won a beauty contest, and then it was all over and they were released into the night.

There were no lights on at the house when they arrived. They had driven back in silence. It was only then that she told him they were to have gone round to the Hawkinses' for a celebration. Her tone was flat, denying him access to her feelings. He put out his hand to touch her arm but she pulled away from him.

'I'll call you in the morning.' she said.

'Can't I come in?'

'Not tonight.'

'What will happen when he comes back? Or will he come back?'

'Nothing will happen. I'll go to bed, that's all.'

He thought to kiss her cheek but the surface was uninviting. She felt like a cold deep lake beside him. He waited until she was inside and the light had come on, then he drove away, back to his hotel.

In his room he switched on the television to catch the late news and took a drink out of the rack of miniatures above the fridge. When he had finished two he picked up his key and walked out into the night again to his car.

Her house was in darkness, and he supposed that, as she had said, she had gone to bed and that nothing would happen. He decided not to go down the driveway in case he frightened her. He had not worked out what he could do, or why he was there. His watch showed midnight. The two hours since prizegiving had finished had slipped by, and he was cold and dazed. He told himself he was crazy, sitting here outside his ex-wife's house, the home of his drunken child, in the middle of the night. A light summer rain had begun to fall, trickling down the windscreen. 'Damn them all to hell,' he said out loud. He jumped, seeing his own ghost, as someone knocked on the window of the car.

It was Stephen. In the pale street light he looked wan and ill, though not incapacitated as he had been in the school hall.

Peter leaned across and opened the door. Stephen slid in beside him.

They sat in silence. 'Well,' said Peter at last.

'I blew it,' said Stephen. For an instant Peter thought his voice sounded humble. On second thoughts he decided that it contained more than the hint of a sneer.

'Blew it!' He knew he sounded shrill, but was unable to stop that, or what he said. 'When have you ever done anything but blow it? I've never seen you unless you were in some sort of trouble or whining or demanding or bullying someone. I thought I was supposed to be seeing a transformation but all I get for a son is a drunken little slob.' He heard himself going on and on, and did not understand what was happening, for he had not travelled to such lengths of anger at least since the days when he lived with Bethany, the terrible days before the end, and the taking of his leave from her and Stephen and Ritchie. Ritchie who was now dead, and this boy sitting here beside him, this Stephen.

Pretty well all that was left, when you came to think about it. His thoughts seemed to be operating at two curious levels. He stopped, waiting for Stephen to go away, to take the final leave. But the boy sat there. Peter wondered if Stephen might hit him, do physical violence upon him. If he were Stephen perhaps that was what he would do.

'You're right, of course,' said Stephen.

Either he or I must be crazy, Peter thought, and yet he was sure he was not mistaken, there was some strange hint of joy in Stephen's voice.

And suddenly Peter understood. This was the first time that he had said what he truly thought to Stephen, spoken without reservation, or careful tact, the language of an estranged father.

After a while Peter said, 'You won the hockey stick.'

'Did I really? I didn't expect that.'

'Fancy you being good at hockey. I used to play, you know.'

'No I didn't. Where did you play? What position?'

'On the wing.'

'That's where I play.'

'Go on now.' The miracle of it overwhelmed Peter. He wanted to weep softly, here in the quiet splattering dark.

'What are you doing sitting here?' Stephen asked.

'I was worried about your mother,' said Peter.

'It's a bit late for that, isn't it?' said Stephen with fresh asperity.

He was entitled to that, Peter thought. 'Why don't we go in together? It might help her,' he said.

Stephen was shocked. 'You can't go in there,' he said.

'Why not?'

Then he saw a car ahead of them parked on the edge of the road that he had not seen through the rain before. He recognised it as Matt's.

Of course, he had known from the moment of his arrival, earlier in the evening.

'I'm sorry,' said Stephen, as if he wished that none of it were so, as if he would like to improve the lot of his parents but was powerless. Which he was, and always had been. If one dared reflect upon that, the meaning of tonight's events might all come clear but that was too difficult and deep to consider. Peter did not think he would ever be up to that.

'Is she happy?'

'You'd have to ask her,' said Stephen.

'Do you mind?'

'Nah. It's nothing to do with me.' He reflected. 'It's not much of a deal for her. He gets all the bikkies, doesn't he?'

'Would you like to come back to Sydney with me tomorrow?' Peter asked on a sudden impulse.

'Do you mean it?' asked Stephen, his face alight in the glow of the car's interior light.

'Of course,' he said stoutly, though even as he spoke, the logistics appalled him. 'I live with a woman called Natalie, she's a dress designer, she's very nice, you'll like her. The flat's a bit small and she works there during the day sometimes, but we'll work something out. It'll be fine.'

Stephen was still. 'I'd like to sometime,' he said carefully.

'You don't want to come?'

'Sure.' But his tone was evasive.

'I may not always live with Natalie, of course,' said Peter. This had just occurred to him, but now he realised that it was true. He was unlikely to live with any woman forever. Once he had thought that he would always live with Bethany, indeed he had vowed to cherish her and protect her as long as they both should live. But that promise had failed and he would never be allowed to redeem it. And if he had been allowed to try, how well could the past be resurrected?

'Can I take a rain check on it?' said Stephen, meaning the invitation.

'Sure, why not?'

'Will you come in, in the morning?' Stephen's face was white and exhausted now, the effects of the alcohol still in their tortuous aftermath.

Peter wanted to say he was goddamned if he would, but even that seemed vain and silly, like all the other things that had brought him and Bethany to this pass. 'I'll have to leave at crack of dawn,' he said, cushioning his refusal. 'Plane to catch. I'll be in touch, okay?'

What did he expect? Suddenly to be called Dad? To be thanked for coming?

Or an embrace?

Yes, there might have been that. He would have liked it.

He slipped the car into gear, thinking that he would work on it.

'Yeah, catch you, mate,' said Stephen, and slid out the door, disappearing into the black.

Puff Adder

I thought I saw Annabel Sherwin in the Pink Gallery viewing the antiques at Dunbar's annual Trentham sale. Afterwards, I had bad dreams.

I had not gone to buy antiques for I could not afford them. But every now and then I am drawn to look at these beautiful objects, despite the vulgarity of some of the would-be buyers. Indeed, I think I go to look at them too, for in their way they are curios of another kind.

The woman I took to be Annabel was standing in front of the Persian rugs. Item 781, to be exact: Shirvan rug with three medallions and stylised birds 4'11" × 3'8", according to the catalogue.

My eyes were full of tears at the time because Ross was with me, and he had complained at the price of the catalogue which he said we did not need if we had not come to buy. But it seemed to me that if we were going to look at the antiques it would be helpful to know what we were looking at and so we had quarrelled like tired foolish children. Ross had bought a catalogue and that had seemed as bad to me as him not buying one. Then he had stood near the door, refusing to look at anything at all.

In January it is very hot in the Pink Gallery. We should probably never have gone. We do not usually behave like that these days. We have come a long way; that is why it was suddenly painful, and I was so close to weeping.

I looked studiously at every item then, as if I was making the best possible use of the catalogue, even though I would have given a lot just to have walked out, I was sick of the whole thing, and sorry for myself too. But because of this careful scrutiny of the catalogue I did know that it was item 781 that Annabel, if it was her, was looking at, and that the Shirvan would have looked exactly right in her long low elegant house in Weyville, the town where we had all lived once, long ago, and where no doubt she did still. It was the house where I believe her son once violated my child, and from which I had been excluded, and asked not to return there, and which, after

100

a period of general humiliation and social ostracism, I had begun to visit again, until I left the town.

I wanted to go over to Ross at once and say, 'Hey, is that Annabel Sherwin over there?'

Of course, as we were not speaking to each other, I didn't.

Besides, on reflection, it is something about which we have nothing more to say.

I walked out of the gallery and caught up with him, already heading back to the car. The sun was harsh and bright.

He took my arm and said, 'Come on Ellen, I'll buy you a drink. Very cold.' It was nice of him and I was grateful.

Still, I couldn't help wondering if he had seen her too.

I cannot imagine Annabel living anywhere else but Weyville; she had a niche there. She had been the queen of our new sub-division many years ago, amongst all the young matrons. Her coffee parties had been at once larger and more exclusive than anybody else's. Larger, because she knew so many people from all over Weyville, not just our suburb; and exclusive because she knew the right people. Living near to Annabel did not always mean that you would be invited, even if you had minded her children for her the Sunday morning before when she and Martin went out for drinks. She had subtle ways of implementing segregation — like telling you that there was measles around, or a new kind of flu, which everyone, or their children, had had but you.

Martin, Annabel's husband, was not a doctor or a dentist or a lawyer, like the husbands of most of her friends. He was, in fact, quite an ordinary clerk in the office of an engineering firm, although Annabel could make it sound as if he was the managing director.

It was Annabel's father who held the key to her good breeding. He had made a fortune out of lavatory pans during the Depression, and now that the industrial magnate's manufacturing days were over the family lived back in Hawke's Bay where their forebears had first settled. I cannot remember who told me about the crap catchers, because it wasn't Annabel, or any of her friends. Still, it was something that everyone somehow knew. She did tell me about Hawke's Bay though. As I got to know her better, she told me more often. I had no doubt that she was well connected. Annabel told me she was, and though it may seem surprising, she was a person who was always believable in her way. Besides, the evidence was in her favour.

Her money didn't bother me, as such. Some people have it, and some don't — in those days my expectations were small. Neither did Annabel herself as a rule, though I was susceptible to hurt. But mostly Ross and I used to joke about her and the silly things she said.

She was exceptionally plain, but she talked about her good looks with such authority that you came to believe in them like everything else about her.

'After I came to Weyville I went for my very first medical to Roland' (she always spoke of doctors by their first name), 'and I took off my dress,' she would say (for she told this story often), 'and there I was in my lovely white satin slip with my boobs swelling up above, and poor Roland took a deep breath and simply didn't know where to look. Annabel, he told me afterwards, I get so many *slags* in here.'

Roland and his wife used to have dinner with Annabel from time to time over the years that followed. I find it difficult to say Annabel and Martin, even though they were such a devoted couple; it is simply that, thinking back, it is hard not to think of Martin as the live-in handyman and not much else in that household, although he could be self-opinionated and pinched bottoms at parties and held forth a lot about what nowadays we call morals campaigning.

I think that today we would describe him as holding double standards.

Annabel would clean her already spotless house for nearly a week before one of these dinner parties, polish silver, organise clothes, set open fires ready for quick combustion, arrange flowers, marinate meat, make sauces, all according to a list that had been made for at least a fortnight before the event. She would also practise smoking, at which she was not accomplished, before her parties. It was still considered smart.

I used to think she looked like a puff adder then, or what I thought a puff adder might look like. I had read that it was 'a deadly snake that blows up the top part of its body when it is excited'. She would puff and blow, filling her plump cheeks with smoke and emitting it in little blue spurts, trying not to cough. At the same time she would attempt to tell racy stories, which nonetheless were never explicit.

All of this would be a rehearsal for Roland's coming. I think it unlikely that they ever slept together. In fact I doubt that

Annabel ever slept with anybody in those days, though she is the sort of woman who is probably coming to it in older age when others of us have learned to care for ourselves.

I return to bad dreams.

When I was a small child I started to have nightmares about snakes. I think they began when my parents taught me how to play snakes and ladders.

In my dreams I would be standing on an island which was only the size of my feet, in the middle of a river. But the river would not be of water, but of snakes.

I carried this dream into adolescence, and although it left me then, the terror of snakes did not. Everything that I disliked I equated with snakes or rats, creatures that slithered near the ground. It is only recently that I have been able to look at snakes on television and only then with the utmost effort of will, and only since the day in an Australian zoo where I had gone for the express purpose of looking at snakes. I walked round and round the snakehouse for nearly an hour that day while school parties of children laughed and shrieked and knocked on the glass at the snakes, before I could bring myself to go up and look at them.

There was an adder with its face pressed against the glass and its eye was open and malevolent, pushed between the soft flesh of its folded body and the pane which parted us. Sick and revolted, I had put my hand against the glass, covering its eye.

I will beat you, I thought then. I will never allow you to terrorise me in my sleep again the way you have all my life.

I thought also, that if there had been an earthquake and the glass had broken, then the snake would have had a chance to win. But the earth was quiet and my luck held, and I do not dream of snakes.

If you asked me, I would say that I looked them in the eye.

Yet I have not stopped dreaming dreams of one kind or another. Maybe it was better when there was a shape. These amorphous shapeless forms are not pleasant either.

Did I see Annabel in the Pink Gallery?

I keep moving away from the point of all this. It is not intentional.

103

Annabel and Martin had three sons. They were very proud of them. You couldn't blame them for that. They were good-looking kids, all dark-skinned with blue eyes and thick eyebrows — I believe Martin's mother was middle European, though just what was never specified. The boys were very charming in their manner. The older two had been trained to wait on table when there were guests, which their friends thought delightful. They freshened up people's drinks, and even complimented Annabel's women friends on their appearance. Their names were Thomas and Humphrey, and the youngest was Adam.

It was a little surprising that Thomas and Humphrey were not at boarding school, but the young people of Weyville were generally cost-conscious and, as well, I suspect that around that time Annabel's brothers had been making demands on the lavatory pan magnate. Besides, between them, most of their friends managed to comprise the local high school board of governors and the school was being run pretty much as they wanted it. They had zoning worked out to suit themselves very well, and most of the Maori kids went to a different school. They had a say in whom the school employed and, as they said, theirs had a good tone. The principal was reputed to be a Christian, practising that is, for Annabel's friends were professed if not always visible ones.

As for us, we occupied a curious geographical position in relation to the Sherwins' house. Several houses were grouped around a park, so that although we were neighbours in the same subdivision, we faced different ways. The Sherwins had been there much longer than we had, and their property had many trees, some old ones which had been left when the division of the land had taken place, others fast growing birches and silver dollars. Their place looked old and established, ours looked new and raw.

And our children, two small girls, were much younger. One was a baby and the other only three, so that there were quite natural barriers to a regular relationship. Indeed, if Adam had not been Annabel and Martin's afterthought, and only four at the time, Annabel and I might have gone month in and month out with nothing more than a wave over the back fence when we were putting out the washing. As it was, Annabel often needed someone to look after Adam during the day, and when I agreed to take him once or twice she offered to take my daughter in return.

I suppose I was grateful. I found suburbia difficult, I never felt that I did it well, I was not good at preserving or bottling, or making the children's clothes. I had started to work on a part-time basis in the evenings, which was frowned upon but gave me a little freedom that saved my sanity. If I was grateful to Annabel, it may even have been for her sillinesses and excesses. I think I found them more amusing than I cared to admit. And although I have dwelt on the ridiculous and pretentious side of her nature, there were times when she seemed kind, and even sensible.

I remember us talking about child molestation one day. 'Ellen,' she said, 'If anyone touched one of my boys I would kill them with my bare hands.'

I was impressed, she spoke with such passion.

I looked at my little girls, and I thought, yes that is exactly how I feel, it is good to have a friend who feels the same way as I do.

Another day, she looked after my three-year-old. She might have to slip out and pick Adam up from afternoon kindergarten, but Humphrey would be home that day, because he had sprained his ankle, and would I mind if he were to keep an eye on my daughter for twenty minutes? He was fifteen after all.

Naturally I said that I did not mind.

My small solemn child was quiet when she came home that day.

The same night she woke crying and I could not comfort her. It took me a long time to understand what she was trying to tell me. At last I did. That afternoon Humphrey had taken her to the gardening shed.

My child was not visibly damaged or hurt, not in the sense of being able to present some evidence. But I do know she was hurt in some other and terrible way. I know that as she grew up her adolescence was blighted by an unnatural reserve, and that though she began to see young men she sometimes appeared to be afraid of them.

Perhaps I interpret events too much in the light of this childhood incident. There may have been the perfidies and quarrels of her parents, a dozen reasons preferably but not easily forgotten, that made her uneasy. Three-year-olds have short memories, you may say. But she says she remembers, and I, who have always claimed early childhood recall for myself, see no reason to deny her the same. The fact is, that for a long time she was unhappy and it is as hard for me, as it has been for her, to see past Humphrey.

And there is more to it than this. There is what we did and didn't do, Ross and I.

For a start, we pretended to our daughter that it had not happened, that it was some figment of her imagination, better forgotten. That was a terrible lie, and it is one of which I am ashamed.

Nor did we at once go to Annabel and Martin. Instead, Ross took time away from his job at the radio station one afternoon and visited the school Humphrey attended, and saw the head-master. It seemed to be the easiest way; we did not want trouble in the neighbourhood and somehow we felt vaguely ashamed of what had happened, as if in some mysterious way we were to blame. We were afraid that we were wrong or would be shown to be wrong, and that that would disturb our careful neigh-bourly relationship.

Yes, that is the truth, we were more concerned about the possi-bility of our lives being disturbed than about getting at the whole truth. To each other we called it 'saving Humphrey's face', or, 'Saving Annabel and Martin'. We did not say, 'saving ourselves'.

The principal was ingratiating to Ross, the worst kind of Christian. He said, yes, he would handle it, he would speak to Humphrey.

Soon after, for the boy's sake, as it was told to us, he also saw Roland, who was on the board of governors. He felt it should be shared with someone who knew the lad, who would help Humphrey, someone who would put him on the right track.

Roland, of course, told Annabel. I think back, and know that was as it was intended. I suppose that it was correct that she should know. She should not have been told this way. That is something that Ross and I did not do well.

If I have a word of defence for my own and Ross's behaviour, it is simply this: Annabel would never have believed whoever told her.

We became, overnight, the neighbourhood outcasts. We were liars and filthmongers. Humphrey's charm was recounted by every indignant matron who had ever enjoyed Annabel's hospitality. Before long no one spoke to me in the supermarket. I changed where I shopped, and was sent a written bill for a loaf of bread that I had put on the slate before the storm.

One evening Annabel rang. Her tone was as cold as the frost on the wires. 'Martin and I have been thinking,' she began. Her voice, beneath its coldness, held the trace of a lisp. I had never noticed it before.

I clung to the phone, my tongue paralysed.

'We really cannot let this situation go on, Ellen,' she was saying. 'We should like to come and see you.'

I thought at first that she was offering to reinstate our friendship.

'There are some things that really ought to be sorted out. You should know where we stand. We're not at all pleased, you know.'

This was a long time ago, twenty years. What does it say of me, of my failures, of my inability to assert myself, of my capitulations, that I went away that night?

Ross suggested that I go to the pictures, and I agreed, though at first I was doubtful. I said, 'It was me she asked, you know.'

But I was the one who went to the school,' said Ross. 'I should sort it out, if that's what they want.'

I was reassured. Confrontations were other people's business. Men's work. Ross would make it all right, and perhaps we would still be friends again.

When I came home that night it had been agreed that our child had made the story up. It was perfectly clear, someone had *talked dirty* — that's what they called it, *talking dirty* — to her and she had rearranged a fiction to fit Humphrey. Our clever little child.

In return, it seemed, life would return to normal, we could go on as we had before, we could all forget. I could belong again.

Nearly, but not quite. It was me that Annabel had wanted the evening she came to visit. Some women seek to punish other people, provided they are never men.

She invited me for coffee a few mornings later. I accepted, and although I was timid when I walked up to her door, I was pleased that she had asked me.

She was practising smoking that morning. Puffing and spurting and erupting in her little clouds of smoke, her prominent eyes glittering.

107

'You'll have to be careful of that child,' she observed, over our second cup of coffee. 'I could tell she was bad from the moment she was born.'

'There are some things she couldn't have known, Annabel,' I ventured.

'Some children are born with dirty minds,' she pronounced. 'Still, if you get onto it early enough you might be able to do something about it.'

I felt humble. She pressed her advantage. 'There had better be no more of this,' she said. 'We can do something about Ross's job, I wouldn't hesitate to go to the top if anything like this comes up again.'

She did not exaggerate; she knew the right people and she could have jeopardised Ross's job. That is how it was then, and maybe still is in Weyville.

I do not know whether it was Annabel in the Pink Gallery. I didn't approach this woman. The chances are, that if I had I would have been civil and charming. That is how people are when they have lived in Weyville and meet years later in the Pink Gallery.

I was sitting in the sun by the sea in a town called Chania in Greece. The sky was a most exquisite and tender blue. From where I was sitting I could see the old sea wall which surrounds the town, jutting out into the sea. A fisherman was laying his nets. Red poppies bloomed in the grass which led to the sand. They were like Flanders poppies, which are part of New Zealand folklore, symbolising death in war; people sell replicas made out of rolled-up red cotton on street corners in April. This was April and the poppies were real.

I was not sure whether the place where I was sitting was on private property or not. It appeared to be the foundations of an old building but it was bare and exposed to the elements, except for the remnants of a thatched roof. It was rather like a derelict pavilion. Alongside of it, and running down to the beach, were steps, which also led to a poor house that stood out on stilts across the water. I knew that it was inhabited, for clothes hung outside, but it is difficult to tell whether buildings are being put up or pulled down in Greece. I sat on a concrete ledge and set about writing to my daughter. The poppies at my feet stirred.

I thought it was a breeze moving amongst them but when I looked, they were alive with rats, foraging in the grass where rubbish had been left. I drew my feet up around me.

'My dear daughter,' I wrote, and stopped. I told myself that it was the sun which made me drowsy, that it was easier just to sit and think of her. I like to think about her. She has turned out funny and clever, tough and wise. She seems not to have suffered a permanent kind of damage. That is what I told myself, sitting in the sun in Greece.

I think I may have gone to sleep, for I did not see the young man come, though he may have passed along the steps beside me, in order to be sitting so close to me, or he may have come from the house below. He was sitting on a rush chair which had been piled in the corner. The chair looked as it if might break under his weight.

'Kalimera,' he said.

'Kalimera,' I responded without warmth.

He smiled, he had bad teeth. I knew that he was thinking that a middle-aged foreign woman sitting alone by the sea in Greece awaited his invitation. Although in New Zealand there are certain Greeks whom I love, in Greece I was uneasy in the presence of local men. I was not afraid the young man would inflict himself on me in a physical way; I mean to say of course that I was not afraid of rape. But I did not wish to have the morning spoiled by his proposition nor bear his displeasure when I refused him.

I tore up the page I had been writing on and started again, in a busy way: 'My dear daughter, my beloved child, there is a language we learn very young, the language of submission, abnegation, guilt, remorse, it is only when we are older that we learn the language of choice. . . .'

Only of course I did not send it. She would have thought that jetlag and loneliness in foreign countries was sending me mad. Besides, she has already learned and unlearned this language, and others that I will never know.

How could it have been that Annabel made me feel responsible for what Humphrey did to my child?

There was another young man, after I left Chania. In London. I was going to lunch at the Grosvenor.

I caught a Victoria Line tube to Green Park, and as I was coming through the subway, a young man died before my eyes.

He had already lain down to die as I arrived at the top of the escalator, and two men were beside him. I stood for a few moments and watched his death. One of the men who had been kneeling by him went for help. I did not like to stand and stare, the young man seemed too dead to be looked at any more.

When I was outside the station I thought that I should have given mouth-to-mouth resuscitation or heart massage. I sat down on a bench and wondered what to do, whether I should go back inside and offer, but so much time had elapsed by then that the situation would certainly have been irretrievable.

I was shocked that I had done nothing. If I had been in New Zealand, I said to myself, I would have done more, I would have been involved. It is all this Britishness that has undone me. That is what I told myself as I went to the Grosvenor for lunch. But I couldn't be certain about it.

When I came home I told my priest this story. 'Ah,' he said, you have discovered that you are not a universal person.' It was a pleasant and priestly way of saying that I had failed to do well enough.

I think he is right. It is easy to make excuses about the circumstances we find ourselves in, and how we react. We can say it was our age, or the times in which we lived, or the place in which we found ourselves. We can perform good acts to expiate the things we did or did not do when we were younger, but there is still something we cannot calculate, which is who we really are, and what we will do when something special is required of us.

Annabel was stronger than me. She had said that she would kill anyone who touched a hair of her children's heads.

She had managed a good deal of damage and embarrassment at our expense, which was perhaps a satisfactory equivalent for Annabel. Whereas I had done nothing about killing Humphrey. Thinking back, it would have been a small thing to do. But leaving even that aside (for, to some, it may seem irrational and extreme), there was a point at which I could simply have stopped agreeing with Annabel. It would have been the very least I could have done for my child.

Hats

L ike turning your hand over, things could go either way with the weather. Six a.m. and the bay is turbulent and green, but at that hour of the morning anything can happen. Standing at the window, just listening, the whole house is a heartbeat. Looking at the bay, the water, the clouds. I think I can hear the busy clink and chatter of the rigging on the boats parked on the hard at the bay, but that can't be right, it's too far away. Oh you can hear anything, see anything on a morning like this, it's the day of the wedding. Our son's getting married.

There is a stirring in the back rooms; there is so much to do, I will never get done, it's crazy this, but the wedding's to be here, not at her place but mine. I am speaking now of the bride's mother and myself. Well, it's a long story, how the wedding comes to be here instead of there, but that's the way it is. She's bringing the food later in the morning, and there'll be crayfish and scallops like nobody ever had at their wedding before, and mussels of course. They are mussel farmers from the Sounds. They. Well I mean the bride's parents.

I love our daughter-in-law to be, I really do. You might think I don't mean that, mothers-in-law rarely do, but it's true. She's a good person. She's loyal. She's had to put up with a few things. Our son's on a win. I want to see him married.

Perhaps they know that. There are times when I think they haven't been so keen. Perhaps they think she could have done better. I don't know. It hasn't been easy, getting this wedding together. But if you knew him, our son, you'd know she wouldn't settle for anyone else. Anyone *less*. Now there's a mother talking, but I've fallen for it, that same old charm of his, and I'll go on forever, I guess. He puts his arms around me, and says, 'Love ya, Ma,' and I'd forgive him anything.

It's true. He brings out a softness in me. That, and rage. But the anger never lasts for long.

There is no time to go on reflecting about it this morning though. There's the smell of baked meats in the air, I need to open up the house and blow it through, I've got the food warmer to collect from the hire depot, and the tablecloths aren't ready, and I have to set up a place for the presents, and there's

111

his mother, that's my husband's, to be got up, and there's relatives to be greeted, and oh God I am so tired. Why didn't anyone tell me I'd be so tired on our son's wedding day, it doesn't seem fair, because I want to enjoy it. Oh by that I mean, I want it all to be right, of course, and I want to do it graciously. We've been at each other a bit over this wedding. Them and us. But I want to make sure it goes all right today. They're bringing the food and the flagons of beer; we're providing the waiters and waitresses in starched uniforms, and the champagne. You have to cater for everyone at a wedding.

Eleven a.m. The food hasn't come. The flagons haven't come. She hasn't come. That's the bride's mother. The wedding is at two. I am striding around the house. The furniture is minimal. We've cleared everything back. There's hardly going to be standing room. That's if there ever is a wedding. There is nothing more I can do. Nothing and everything. If only we had another day. It would be better if we had held off another month. The weather would have been better. Not that it's bad but the breeze is cold. It'll be draughty in the church.

The church, ah, the church. It looks so beautiful. The flowers. They are just amazing. Carnations and irises, low bowls of stocks . . . there are the cars now, all the relatives bearing trays and pots and dishes, straggling up the stairs. The food looks wonderful. God, those crays, there's dozens of them. I'm glad they've done the food, I could never have done it so well. And the cake. Our daughter-in-law-to-be's auntie has made the cake and it's perfect too.

Everyone's exhausted, it's not just me, they've been up all night. Still, I wish they could have got here a bit sooner and we all have to get dressed yet. It's cutting things fine. I feel faint, even a little nauseous, as if lights are switching on and off inside my brain. She can't be as tired as I am, nobody could be that tired. How am I going to make it through the rest of the day?

'I'd better be getting along,' says the auntie to the bride's mother. 'I've still got to finish off your hat.' The aunt has a knack with things, clothes and cakes, she's the indispensable sort.

Inside me, something freezes. 'Hat,' I say, foolishly, and in a loud voice. 'You're wearing a hat?'

There is a silence in the kitchen.

'Well, it's just a little hat,' she says.

'You said you weren't going to wear a hat.' I hear my voice, without an ounce of grace in it, and I don't seem to be able to stop it. There is ugliness in the air.

The auntie, her sister, says, 'She needed a hat to finish off the outfit. It wouldn't look right without it.'

'But we agreed,' I say. 'You said you couldn't afford a hat, and I said, well if you're not wearing one, I won't.'

The silence extends around the kitchen. She fumbles a lettuce leaf, suddenly awkward at my bench.

'It's all right,' I say, 'it's nothing.' My face is covered with tears. I walk out, leaving them to finish whipping the cream.

'Where are you going?' my husband says, following at my heels.

'Out. Away.'

'You can't go away.'

'I have to. I'm not going to the wedding.'

'No, stop, don't be silly.' He's really alarmed, I'm right on the edge, and he's right, I might go off at any moment and make things too awful for everyone to endure. At the rate I'm going there mightn't be any wedding.

'Come into the shed,' he says, speaking softly, like a huntsman talking down a wild animal. 'Come on, it'll be all right. You're tired, just tired.'

I follow him. Inside the toolshed I start to cry properly. 'I want a hat,' I say. 'I wanted to wear a hat all along, but I promised her. I promised I wouldn't get a hat.'

'I'll get you a hat. Come along, we'll go into town and buy you a hat.'

'It's too late, the shops will be shut.'

'We could just make it to James Smith's,' he says. But it is too late, I can see that. Even if we broke the speed limit I'd only have five minutes, it being Saturday. The shops were due to close in half an hour.

'I can't go without a hat. What'll I do?'

'You'll think of something,' he says. 'You always do. Hey, we can do anything, can't we?' He pulls my fists out of my eyes. 'What can we do? We can . . .' He waits for me to join in the refrain with him.

'We can walk on water if we have to,' I chant.

But I'm not sure how I will.

Back in the kitchen everyone is tiptoeing around. 'It looks wonderful,' I say heartily. 'Just great. Don't you think you should be getting along. I mean, if you're going to get dressed?'

They nod. They are not deceived, but they are glad to be excused. They have been afraid to take their leave in my absence.

They are gone, and our son and his best man are dressed, preening in their three-piece suits. Oh they are so handsome. It calms me, just seeing them. As for him, I want to stroke and stroke him. My boy. In a suit. Oh I'm square. When it all comes down to it. But he's proud of himself too.

'Y'okay, Ma?'

He doesn't know what's been going on, but he sees I'm pale.

'Of course I'm okay,' I say, and for his sake I must be. I must also have a hat.

I ring our daughter. 'What about all those hats you bought when you were into hats?' I ask. I think of the op shops where she has collected feathered toques and funny little cloches. I have a feeling that none of them will suit me. She is so tall and elegant. 'I think they're in the baby's toybox,' she says.

'Have a look,' I command.

'God, I've got to get dressed too.'

'Have a look.'

I hold grimly onto the phone. She comes back. 'There's three, the black one with three feathers, and the sort of burgundy one, and the beige one with the wide brim.'

'That's it, the beige one. I'm sending Dad over for it right now.'

'But Mum.'

'It'll be all right. Well, look I can try it anyway.'

'But Mum.' This time she gets it out. 'The baby's been sick on it.'

'How sick?'

'Really sick.'

No one is going to put me off now. I think she is conspiring with the odds to stop me making a fool of myself. I won't let her save me, though. 'Dad'll be right over,' I say.

But it's true. The baby has been very sick on the hat. I'm sure our daughter shouldn't have put it back in the toybox like that. I resolve to speak to her about it at some later date.

In the meantime there is work to be done. I fill the sink with hot soapy water and get out the scrubbing brush. In a few moments the sick has gone. I have a soggy felt hat dripping in my hands, but at least it is clean.

The husband and wife team, 'available for cocktail, waitressing and barman duties in the privacy of your own home', has arrived. 'Don't worry about a thing,' they say. 'You just enjoy yourselves and we'll take care of everything from now on.'

In the clothes drier, the hat whirls around.

Our son has left for the church. Soon we'll have to go too. My husband is resplendent. He wears his father's watch chain across his waistcoat. His father was a guard on the railways, back in the old days. That watch has started a thousand trains on country railway stations. Sometimes I remonstrate with my husband for wearing it; it doesn't always seem appropriate. Today it is exactly right. The spring in the watch has given up long ago, but the watch will start the wedding on time. Sooner or later.

My hands shake so much he has to do up the pearl buttons on my Georgia Brown silk. 'It's time we were going,' he says tentatively. I know he's thinking about the hat, and wondering if he can get me away without it.

But it's dry. Dry, and softly drooping around the brim, so that it swoops low over my right eye when I put it on. I stare at myself in the mirror, entranced. I feel beautiful. I glow. I love hats. This hat is perfect.

Our son's wife-to-be is late, but then she usually is. Anyone is allowed one failing. I don't mind. It gives me time to relax, breathe deeply, smile and wave around the church. Across the aisle I see her, the mother of the bride. She is not wearing a hat.

Instinctively, I touch the brim of mine. I have shamed her into coming without her hat. I should feel jubilant but I don't. I feel bad, wonder how to take mine off without drawing attention to myself. But it's impossible. At the door to the church the priest has said, first thing when he sees me, 'Oh what a beautiful hat.'

I look away, embarrassed. I tell myself I must not think about it. The wedding is about to happen, and we can't repeat it when I'm feeling better, so I've just got to stop thinking about it, the hat on my head.

And then they're there, coming into the church together, which is what's been arranged, and it's not quite the same old responses, because some of that wouldn't be suitable, but they say some nice things to each other, making promises to do things as well as they can, and they're so young, so very young, and that's all you can expect from anybody, to do their best, isn't it?

The couple are facing the congregation now. This really is very modern. Our daughter stands up at the lectern and reads from the Book of Ecclesiastes, and then some Keats, *O brightest! though too late for antique vows*, and she's pale and self-contained and not showing signs of things turning over inside of her, and so lovely; she and the boy, her brother, look at each other, and it's as if they're the only ones in the church for a moment, *Holy the air, the water, and the fire*, like a conversation just for the two of them, putting aside all their childish grievances, though a few people in the church who haven't done English Lit. look a trifle confused but it doesn't matter, these two know . . . *so let me be thy choir . . . thy voice, thy lute, thy pipe . . .* and then our son and his new wife's baby cries at the back of the church where he's being held by the auntie, and the spell's broken, as the two parents look anxiously after their child. The wind rises in the funnel where the church stands, and a plane roars overhead, and the light shines through the stained glass window onto the same spot where my father's coffin stood last year, and with all the light and the sound I don't hear any more of the service, I just smile and smile.

It's over. We're forming up to leave. She and I look at each other across the church again. Suddenly it's all bustle and go, and what none of us have thought about is the way we get out of the church, but there it is, as old as the service itself, or so it seems, the rituals of teaming up, like finding your partner for a gavotte, step step step an arm offered and accepted she goes with my husband and I go with hers, that's the way it's done. Delicate, light as air, we prepare our entrance to the dance, to the music, but before we do, she and I afford each other one more look, one intimate glance. Hatted and hatless, that's us, blessed are the meek, it's all the same now. We're one, her and me. We're family.

Needles and Glass

Again she watched the women walk across the grass towards the man. They smiled and some of them laughed aloud. There were so many of them. The man's eyes were dark and watchful, his cheekbones jutted above his beard. Then Helena's father hurried her away so that she could not watch them any more. Only, that night, the wind carried the voices of the women to her. They spoke a language she did not understand.

Around her now was the night, and in the bed before her was the dying woman. Helena felt the dark around them and the wind pressed against the window pane. There were pockets of silence in the hospital and yet they were not silences if you listened with all your senses. Sounds leaned in. The sluicing room where the bedpans were cleaned was down the corridor. Spasmodic jets of water hissed on the enamel. Pans clattered together as they were picked up. Helena got up from the bedside and walked down the corridor, her feet gliding on the brown linoleum.

'Nurse Moore.'

The young woman carrying the pans stopped and did not turn.

'Yes, Sister?'

'Look at me when I speak to you.'

The young woman turned to face her. 'I'm sorry, Sister,' she said, before Helena had spoken again. 'Mrs Carrington's flooding.'

Her hands shook slightly as she clasped the pans. A wedding ring glinted on the left hand. Her face was fair and pretty, but tired, her hair greasier than it should have been and straggling from under her cap.

'Move quietly, how many times must I tell you . . . Well go then, if you're needed.'

Nurse Moore began her journey down the corridor again. 'And see me in the morning before you go off duty.' said Helena.

The nurse cast a quick agonised glance over her shoulder, her eyes beseeching, and walked on.

And why did I do that, Helena wondered. Who's to gain,

when an exhausted woman waits back for a reprimand which I have not even composed, while her children wait for their breakfast and their father is about to leave in search of work again?

Ah, the unemployed. Like beggars at the door. They had fed ten of them that night and God knows where they were sleeping now. At least Moore and his wife had a roof over their heads, and some thanks to her for that too, keeping Moore on, for she was a nurse of only average capability. No, standards must not slip, she had no reason to reproach herself.

Back at her vigil, she thought to lean her face against the window, but stopped herself. She expected better discipline than that from her staff. Was she not Helena McDonald McGlone, with a standard to set? We are the best, her father had told her, we are from a proud line, we own castles, we are lairds among our own, we must not forget it here.

The hospital was on a high hill and the sea was below. There were no stars and she thought she heard a storm rising out beyond the harbour reef. A light jerked far below her and it seemed to be on the water. The ships, like the poor, were restless. How the hungry wandered, not just now, but always. They would stop at the farmhouse door, and the servants would give pitchers of water to the swaggers, and sometimes her mother would come out to buy soap, or pins, or some herbal remedy from the passers-by. Why did she buy things she would never use, Helena would ask her, and her mother, delicate as the silk roses she sewed on her cushions, would sigh and say that they must help the poor. Won't we be poor too, if we help too many of them, Helena had asked then, but her mother had shaken her head at such cosmic incomprehensibility, and told her that they must do what they could to relieve the sufferings of others.

Which was more or less why she was here, Helena supposed. Only lately the poor seemed to have increased. It occurred to her that Nurse Moore was pregnant. She couldn't understand how she had failed to notice this before, or why she had happened to notice on this particular evening, for that matter.

Something to do with the way she had straightened her back and turned carefully when Helena had spoken, perhaps. Helena sighed, thinking about it. There would be nothing else for it. It was so difficult, the way things were going, and the riots and the looting in the towns. She hoped Moore's husband would keep his head. Oh but if the fool had kept other things under control.

She wrapped her arms around her. It had become colder in the room.

And the dark women moved over the grass again and the land was covered with light. The sun beat fiercely and the beads they wore twinkled and shone. The man was impassive as they came to him, but his eyes seemed to single out one of them.

Which one had it been, which one?

Some of them sang that night in the woolshed where her father let them stay, before their journey north began again next day. The man helped her father to dig a ditch in return for their food and shelter. It was hard work in heavy clay and it had tired her father a great deal. Was the man tired too, and did he, that night, lie down to rest as her father had done, quietly, and in a separate room from her mother, who lay in the double bed with her fine hair spread upon the lace-edged pillowslip? She knew that he did not. There were no separate rooms in the woolshed, only bare boards and the deep and greasy smell of sheep fleece.

Which one? Why did the others sing?

The crumpled body in the bed before her now was stirring. Helena reached to pull up the covers, thinking that the cold must have woken her patient. But by the light from the corridor, Helena could see that the eyes were wide and unnaturally bright. She switched on a night-light. There was a syringe of morphine on the table beside the bed. The table was lustrous and bare except for the small tray holding the syringe. Helena expected she would have to use it before the dawn. It was only two o'clock now, and it was too soon.

But when the pain came, it bit hard and with only the briefest warning, and though the woman would fight against it, once it began she would scream, and the hospital ring with the sound of agony.

'Is the pain coming, Mrs Hardcastle?'

'I'm not sure.'

'Tell me if you need an injection.'

'You'd let me have it?'

'If you need it.'

'If I need it?' For a moment the voice was waspish. 'Since when did I decide when I needed it?'

When Helena didn't answer, she said, 'Then it's as I thought.'

'What did you think?' said Helena.

'Oh, you know, that it'll happen soon.' Her fingers plucked the sheet. 'I'll be glad, you know.'

'I expect so.'

'You expect so, eh? That's a strange thing to say. As if you'd like me to. Well, why not, I can't say I blame you, you've put up with me long enough.'

'No, it's not that. I expect you're tired of this, that's all.'

'Yes, that's true, I'm tired all right.'

Mrs Hardcastle was silent awhile, frowning to herself. Far away, in another part of the hospital someone began to shriek. Both women cocked their heads.

'Shouldn't you be there?' the patient asked.

'The doctor's with her.'

'Such a fuss some of them make. Oh I'm not one to talk, I suppose you'd say, look at all the noise I've made. But babies, that's a different matter . . . no dignity some of them.'

'No two are the same.'

'You'd know I suppose.'

Helena caught sight of her reflection in the glass, illuminated by the night-light, and it occurred to her that she knew nothing at all. Her face was pale but then that was always so, her eyes nearly as black as her hair: a McGlone, her father had said, with approval. Yet in this strange night her image on the glass might have belonged to anyone, even one of the women who walked across the grass.

Outside the wind was dropping and a prickle of stars emerged from behind the clouds. If the night could have penetrated the room it would be full of frost now, and not a storm at all. By this new light a shadow moved. It would be the beggars, searching for food. Helena remembered then her mother's dying and the moustache which grew on her finely moulded upper lip before the end, where food and saliva would gather, and it had become so hard to kiss her once-beautiful face.

'Will I get someone for you?' Helena asked.

'Is it as close as that, d'you think?'

Helena took the woman's pulse, so that it was some time before she answered. 'It's difficult to tell,' she said at last. 'Have you still no pain?'

'No,' said her patient. 'It seems to be taking a rest.' She touched the spread covering her distended stomach, speaking of the tumour as if it were a live creature, apart from her.

'You can have the morphine if you want.'

'Thank you. But let's wait and see what it thinks.' She touched the coverlet again.

'And you don't want anyone?'

Mrs Hardcastle was not very old, or certainly not old enough for it to be said that her time had come. Helena had forgotten exactly how old, although she had seen it on the records, but she knew she was closer to sixty than seventy. Her hands were thick and even after months in hospital there was still a roughness about them from scrubbing with cold water, and helping out on the farm when her son's wife was in having babies. She and the man she called Dad, or Jack, depending on how she was feeling about him after a visit, still took their turn on the farm. Helena supposed that in a sense she must still have a role to play there, to help out like that while the next generation were being born and raised. There was a useful place in the world that she would leave empty with her death. Helena wondered if that could be possible in her own life. It seemed unlikely. There would be other nursing sisters to run small country hospitals, the world was full of unmarried women who did their work well.

'He's got to do the milking this morning, it wouldn't be fair,' said the patient, coming to a decision.

'But . . .' Helena checked herself, it felt like giving special leave to one of the staff to attend a wedding or a ball.

Mrs Hardcastle was almost apologetic. 'Young Rob had to go to town overnight, see. The separator broke down. You can't be without the separator.'

'No, of course not.'

'It'll be all right. You'll stay, won't you?'

'Oh yes.'

'Besides, it mightn't be till after the milking.'

'Shall I put the light off?'

'It doesn't make much difference. No, leave it on.'

For a long time then, they sat in silence. Mrs Hardcastle appeared to doze and didn't move when Nurse Moore came to tell Helena that Mrs Carrington had given birth to a daughter and was safe. The doctor put his head in the door a little later, and took Mrs Hardcastle's pulse and temperature, and still she drowsed on without seeming to notice. Out in the corridor Helena told him what had taken place, and he said the patient might last until the morning or longer, who knew, she was closer to death than either of them and might know more about it. He said he would sleep at the hospital if Helena wished, but he was white with exhaustion, and besides she had the needle on the shining table, and she sent him away. Somewhere out on the rim of the world the light would be weaving its way towards them, but still it was not dawn. Now Helena knew that there was indeed a frost outside, and she thought how hard it would be for Jack Hardcastle as he faced the milking alone in another hour or so. Now that the wind had dropped she knew it could not be the trees that moved outside but surely there were not so many of the poor out there roaming the night either. There were too many shapes. She rubbed her eyes. The women were moving again, only this time they were moving towards her. Their hands were empty but there seemed to be something bounteous about them, as if they carried fruit and flowering branches. One of them held her hands in front of her as if she was holding melons but then Helena saw that it was her breasts she was holding high.

'What time is it?' asked Mrs Hardcastle.

Helena jumped, trembled. 'Nearly five o'clock,' she said.

The palest sliver of light was slitting the sky.

'Could I have half the needle now?' said Mrs Hardcastle. Her breath was panting quietly.

'You can have it all.'

'No . . . I want to be awake when it comes . . . aah, yes, yes. Thank you, Sister, you're a good girl, yes.'

'Lie back now; it's all right, I'm here with you.'

But Mrs Hardcastle's hand had floundered towards the table where Helena had replaced the now half-empty syringe.

'What is it?' Helena asked.

'My spectacles. Will you put them on me, please?'

'Why yes, if you want.'

She hooked the steel frames around Mrs Hardcastle's ears and propped the bridge as comfortably as she could on her thin nose.

'What do you see?' she asked, for Mrs Hardcastle was peering around her in a distracted way.

'I don't know. Everything and nothing. You can see so much and still do nothing about it, can't you?'

'I suppose so. Yes, I'm sure you're right.'

'I've seen a lot of things in my time. Too late to tell you now. Should have. Would you have been interested? Would you have listened?'

'Of course.'

'Ah, would you though? Tell me, Sister, what have you seen?'

'Oh . . . I don't know. Not much. The things that have happened in hospitals, sick people, things like that you know.'

'Oh that, yes I can see that. But I mean, what have you seen? Really seen?'

Helena walked to the window again and thought, I should not be having this conversation, I am a nurse, it is not for me to tell people about myself, my private self. And yet, what did it matter, in a few hours this would all be over, there was nothing to lose. Her face closer to the glass, the reflection full of fine lines. No girl this, a woman growing older; soon she would be middle-aged, and then before you could turn around, an old woman like the one in the bed beside her, if she made it that far. She reached back into her memory for something she might have seen that this woman had not. The McGlones and the McDonalds, perhaps, but they were only her parents and, if it came to that, maybe not quite so different as they would have had her believe.

'I saw the women,' she heard herself say.

'The women, what women?' mumbled the figure on the bed.

'Rua's women, I saw Rua Kenana.'

'Rua, the one they called the prophet? He was a bit of a madman, wasn't he?'

'Oh, who knows. They called him a mystic man too, a messiah. You do know who I mean?'

'Oh yes.'

'He'd travel the land with his band of many wives, looking for work on the farms. Well, he stayed a night at my father's farm and his wives were with him. He worked alongside my father, and at night they slept in the woolshed. All together, you understand?'

'Yes, I understand,' said Mrs Hardcastle.

'They wore beautiful hats and finery. Later, I heard that he built them a house with many rooms . . . for all the wives . . . and the children . . . Afterwards, they captured Rua, took him away. You can understand that he would make people angry, I suppose. So many wives.'

Mrs Hardcastle's breath came out in a long sigh from the bed. Helena glanced at her, suddenly afraid that her companion would leave her too soon, before they were done.

But, 'What were the wives really like?' Mrs Hardcastle asked.

'I can't tell you. I wasn't allowed to go near them. Or not near enough to be sure of anything,' Helena said.

'You must have seen something.'

'Well, I don't know for sure . . . but I think they were happy.'

Helena saw that the sky was now full of delicate pale light. Mrs Hardcastle mumbled something she could not understand.

'What did you say?' Helena gasped, bending close to her, for now it was imperative to know what the other woman thought about all of this. She had never told anyone before, never shared such confidences. Mrs Hardcastle mumbled again. Helena leaned nearer.

'I expect Jack'll come after the milking.' The words were deathly quiet.

The new day took over and possessed the room, and Helena began the last work on her shift, methodical, tidying up as she went. When she had done all there was to do, and spoken to everyone, and given comfort to the bereaved, then remembered to give Nurse Moore a month's notice, she let herself into her room in the adjacent nurses' home. She turned the key in her lock and sank down on the narrow bed, easing off her shoes as she did so. She was thoughtful as she pulled out the trunk beneath the bed and opened it. Inside the trunk, among her summer clothes stored away for the next season, there lay an assortment of items. They included several syringes and twenty or thirty pairs of spectacles. From her pocket she took the pair of spectacles which Mrs Hardcastle had worn, folded now in a narrow red case, and the half-empty syringe. For a moment she thought of throwing the syringe away, for what use was half a needleful to anyone? But there was so much waste around, and one never knew when any of it might come in handy. She tossed the spectacle case and the syringe in with the others, and when she had closed the trunk, lay down at last, to sleep.

Body Searches

'Wellington is like a Jane Austen novel,' says Alberto. He stands looking out the window with his back turned against Cushla, so that he cannot see her dressing, for which she is grateful, even while it rankles that he makes so little attempt to hide his lack of interest in her body now that they have completed the act he has so recently pursued with such determination.

'You mean it's a backwater?' she says, struggling into her brassière and blouse. As she had undressed she had thought how foolish it was to wear a garment with so many buttons, for what, after all, is an assignation for sex. But it occurs to her that she may have chosen the blouse with greater deliberation than she realised, as if by wearing something difficult and fussy she might still avert the inevitable. For it is like this with Alberto. She does not wish to go to bed with him but his insistence wears her down. Like other women who have had affairs and become tired of them, of the intrigue, of the fear of discovery, of the endless planning which goes into illicit relationships, she nevertheless finds the familiar difficulty in refusing, of saying no. It is something her generation has not been trained to do; no matter how many assertiveness training courses they go to, the lessons never seem to stick. It is impossible to say no to sex without giving offence and she, who administers offence with easy matter-of-factness in her regular daily life, is not capable of offending men who want to sleep with her. Well, those whom she classes as friends, at least.

'Something like that, it's certainly behind the times,' says Alberto. He is still naked to the waist. He glances over her briefly, then turns back to the window. His dark moustache droops at the corners, giving him a sad, slightly regretful appearance. She pulls her half-slip hastily up over her hips so that she appears clad over all her parts.

'You've spent too much time in that dreary hole of yours.' She means London. Alberto is a television producer with whom she attended university when they were both very young. He was serious and withdrawn in those days, with an accent that still held rough traces of English spoken as a second language. Everyone was aware then, although it was not said, that sacrifices were made for him to go to university. Somebody would go without, or work even longer hours than they already did, in order that Alberto should receive a higher education. Sometimes he would have a slight odour of fish about him. He was called Albie in those days, though now of course he is known by his given name. Nobody had been able, had dared to say no to Alberto, then. It might have ben construed as snobbish or discriminatory. We were all so liberal, thinks Cushla with sudden bitterness. Look what it's done for us. For me anyway. I still can't say no to Alberto. Thank God he only comes here once a year.

For Alberto returns annually to spend two months with his daughters, who have long since returned to New Zealand with their mother, with whom both he and Cushla were also at university. The mother's name is Rosemary, and Cushla hasn't seen her in years. She has remarried, to a dentist, Cushla thinks, though she can't be sure. Alberto was her mistake, or perhaps, like Cushla, she too had been unable to say no.

Although encounters in bed with Alberto are a recent complication in her life. An accidental meeting in the street, a cup of coffee, an invitation to call by and collect a book that he had recommended, and to meet his daughters, which, put the way he did, could not be refused. Not without giving offence. The daughters are out when she calls.

What happens between them is a mistake, he says afterwards when she tells him that she does not have affairs. It was lovely but it won't happen again, he swears. He understands how she feels absolutely.

Now he calls every time he is in town. He is entirely plausible in his invitations. The daughters are always out. It is hard to be alone in one's own hometown, he says. You are not alone, she argues every time, you still have friends here.

But not like you, he says, and his eyes are reproachful. Just come and see me, that's all I ask.

'Wellington's not a backwater,' she says irritably now, 'it's the most interesting city in New Zealand. Look at how it's changed.' She hasn't meant to say this for she does not really approve of the glass façades which have sprung up all along Lambton Quay, the glitzy malls and the enormous price one pays for a cup of coffee in the transparent galleries. At least she tells people she doesn't because her left-wing sensibilities are offended, but she has long suspected that she is more than a little attracted to it all. No wonder she has such difficulty saying no to Alberto. She is not positive enough in her convictions.

'It is not so much how it looks,' says Alberto, 'it is what it is. Such minor matters assume the dimensions of catastrophes.'

Looking in the mirror, replacing her make-up, Cushla is silent. Perhaps he is right. Her own catastrophe looks back at her. She has grown deeply lined over the past year and her throat is in a state of collapse. Her perm (or body wave, as they call it now) is dried out and she needs to make an appointment for an oil treatment. She applies her make-up with the critical concern of someone attending the ill.

But the news is not all bad. You have such nice eyes, people say, such wide eyes. They are as dark blue as it is possible for eyes to be; in certain lights at night, they have an inky quality. They shine back at her from the glass, bright and mocking. She pins her silk scarf in place, and collects her leather shoulder bag.

'You'll get cold standing there,' she says to Alberto. In fact it is warm outside but she cannot think of anything else to say to him, and she wishes he was dressed. His chest is narrow and vulnerable and she suspects that he might use this slight fragility as a lever when proposing another meeting, to make a fresh assignment. He makes a half-hearted gesture of pulling her towards him as she leaves, but she avoids him. His mouth is soft and his damp kisses pressed on her skin have never been part of his attraction. If she analyses it, there is nothing about him that appeals. She is shocked; she has been telling herself that there must be something, or she wouldn't have come back a second and third time this year. But there is nothing, except for his sorriness for himself, and she is ashamed.

'When will you come again?' he says.

'I don't know. It's difficult to get away,' she mutters, still playing the role of the scheming lover.

He nods sympathetically. 'You will stay married to that fellow. I'll call you.'

It is winter when Cushla goes to the doctor. She has dressed carefully in a dark blue and pink dress with a paisley pattern and a ruffled bodice. She has bought new patent leather shoes, and a complete set of new underwear. Altogether, she has spent a long time wavering over the image she wishes to project, trying to strike a balance. On the one hand she feels she should look smart and worldly, but then she does not want her appearance to suggest that she is without conscience about her problem. What she has chosen seems correct for the occasion, suggesting that she is nice, and, she hopes, at the same time, that she is a serious kind of woman.

'What is your occupation, Mrs Grayson?' asks the doctor as he fills in a form, immediately giving her the opportunity to tell him that she is, indeed, a woman of intelligence and responsibility.

'Deputy principal. I'm a teacher,' she adds unnecessarily.

He raises his eyes and looks at her over the top of his fine-rimmed spectacles, then sits back in his chair.

Cushla looks at the floor and feels her face going crimson. Dr Gilroy seems like a nice man, which in a way is worse than if he was unpleasant or officious or very young. She has not been able to face going to her own doctor who is very young and often complains about the number of women he has to see who are middle-aged and neurotic with all the aches in the world yet rarely suffer complaints that can be diagnosed. Now she has arrived at this age herself and she lives in terror of having to tell him her ailments. Look, she wants to say to him, I am full of fear, and I know that if I had been ill for as long as I have been afraid, I would probably be dead by now, but still, what I have to tell you is important. She is especially frightened that he will find nothing wrong with her, even though she wants to live forever. But now there is nothing she wants more than that Dr Gilroy will find that she is in good health. Dr Gilroy is a specialist whose name she has found in the phone book.

He speaks gently. 'What is the problem, Mrs Grayson?'

She tries to speak but she is overwhelmed by the difficulty of it all.

After a moment or two has elapsed he tries to help her again. 'You see,' he says, shifting in his chair, 'sometimes, when women like yourself come to me, it is hard for them. Women are so loyal to their husbands. Even when they do . . . err, perhaps?'

'Oh no,' says Cushla quickly. Too quickly. Good God, she thinks, who says men are to blame for everything? She cannot avoid the truth any longer. 'It's me that's erred,' she says humbly. 'I . . . it was just the once. Well, once or twice. I . . .' Her voice trails away. It would perhaps have been easier to go to the clinic after all. She cannot imagine what it would really be like but, in her mind's eye, she is sure that there are rows of institutional chairs, and brown walls, and that the inhabitants of such a waiting room are transvestites and girls from the massage parlours. She has considered herself to be above all that. But now, looking at the kindly grey-haired man, she thinks that she should have stuck amongst her own kind, that the clinic would more properly have been the place for her to go. If she is going to be pulled down a peg or two she really ought to go along with everyone else who has erred. At least these people of her imagination had purpose in the act which inspired their condition. Money, companionship, who knew, even desire. Whereas she was paying for no more than a failure of will, and an inability to relinquish a slight frivolousness in her nature.

'Well, that's no great harm done, surely,' says Dr Gilroy.

'It would be if I . . . well, if I had a disease.'

'What makes you think you have a venereal disease?'

She thinks back to the summer when they have all been to the beach, a week or two after the last time with Alberto. The cottage that she and her sister and their husbands have taken each year, for as long as they can remember, was bursting with people. Their children (six between the two families), who rarely came together now except for the annual holiday, had appeared with even more hangers-on than in the past, as if their independence from home meant that they felt free to inflict more people on their parents each time they saw them. The bunk-house was full and there were tents pitched all round the cottage. At one stage Cushla and Margaret had counted sixteen people at breakfast. Cooking sufficient fish over the coal range to fill them all had taken until ten o'clock. 'Whoever said it was a holiday?' Margaret remarked as they both climbed into bathing suits, and started smoothing suntan lotion on their shoulders.

'Was it ever? Did we ever really believe it?' Cushla had replied. It was then, as she eased her bathing suit around her crotch, that she noticed the lump. It was smooth and hard like a long flat pebble. Her fingers stopped at it, silently querying its presence.

She had spent a lot of time in the sea over the next few days, floating on her back with her eyes closed. She was uncertain what the lump might be, and thought more of cancer than of anything else. That was what one thought when alien lumps appeared. She composed obituaries for herself, and wondered whether the school would hold a memorial service for her.

After the holiday she returned to school early to help with the timetable, and when the school year began the lump had disappeared.

'And that was all?' probes Dr Gilroy.

'He said, the man said, that it was me. You know, that I had given it. To him. It wasn't possible. Truly.'

When Alberto had rung it was four o'clock in the morning. Philip had lifted the phone with weary impatience, assuming a wrong number, while she had fretted on the other side of the bed, imagining one of the children was hurt.

'It's for you. London,' Philip said as he passed her the phone. He was wide awake, looking at her with a sharp question in his expression.

'So thanks a lot,' Alberto was screaming on the other end of the line. 'Thanks for the dose of pox, lady.'

'You got the times wrong, Alberto,' Cushla had said brightly. 'It's four o'clock here. Four in the morning.'

'I don't care what goddamn time it is, why the fuck should I care what time it is, I tell you I got a mother fuckin' disease.'

'That's wonderful,' Cushla said, 'really great news, but why don't you call me about it later when I can think straight?'

'Jesus, woman, don't you hear what I say?'

'Have a glass of champagne for me, clever boy.'

She had put the phone down and rolled over in bed. 'Sorry,' she had said to Philip. 'It was Alberto, the fool doesn't seem to know what time it is.'

'What did he want?'

'He's just landed some big contract. I couldn't follow him.'

'Why did he ring you?'

'He's drunk. Go back to sleep.'

'You've got funny friends.'

'So what did you do?' Dr Gilroy asks.

'Nothing.'

'Nothing?' He looks pained, for the first time.

'I knew I couldn't have. I mean, I really knew. What happened to me, it was an accident. You must believe me.'

He nods. 'I do believe you. And, Mrs Grayson, even if I didn't, I'm not here to judge you, you know.'

'No. Thank you. I can see that. But what I did, it was very foolish.' Looking at her hands she notices how freckled they have become, and how the skin collects in folds around the knuckles. It is our hands that give us away, she thinks. She flexes them in her lap, bony hands with fingertips which curve upwards slightly when she stretches them. She played the piano when she was younger, talks often of playing it again. 'After a while I began to think, well, if he's sick now, perhaps he was when I saw him. I couldn't get rid of the thought. Later, I came out in a rash. Oh I know what you're thinking, but it was months after. Just a blotchy raised rash. On my arms and legs. I thought, maybe something I'd eaten.'

'Was it true?' she had asked Alberto on the phone. 'Did you really have a disease?'

'Of course I didn't, pet,' he had murmured. 'You didn't believe that, did you?'

'Then why did you say so, Alberto, why, it's been tearing me apart, what if I had it? What if you had given it to me, or if I had given it to Philip?'

'But my love,' and he sounded easier and more accomplished in his manner than he ever did in Wellington, 'I didn't.'

'But you said.'

'I know, I was drunk.'

Although she had told Philip that he was, it had never occurred to her that in fact, he might have been.

'We get older,' he had said, 'the plumbing goes wrong, you know. It was a temporary indisposition. Forgive me,' he said, contrite. 'I want to see you again. I'll come back to New Zealand soon. Just a few more months.'

'No, Alberto. I've finished seeing you.'

'There you see, you're angry with me. Well,' and his voice rose a note or two. 'I was angry too. You promised you'd come and you didn't. I love you, you know, Cushla, always loved you, never should have married Rosemary. Ah.' His sigh was extravagant. 'The mistakes we make in our youth.'

'You. You loved me? Oh Albie. Love!'

She had put the phone down in his ear, and for nights afterwards regretted it, for fear that he would ring her again in the night.

And her rash itched.

After a while it went away too.

'Mrs Grayson, syphilis is very rare in this country now. About one in a hundred thousand cases of reported venereal disease turn out to be syphilis here these days.'

'He . . . he leads a different lifestyle. In another country.'

'He isn't a male prostitute, is he?'

'Oh but good heavens no . . . He's an old friend. I've known him for years.' She pauses. 'But he has changed,' she says, reflecting.

'Not gay? Bisexual? We have to consider Aids now.'

'I shouldn't think so. I don't know. You never know now, do you?'

She saw him at a concert with a girl just before he was due to return to London. He hadn't seen her. Alberto would always be seen with women. But did that mean he always kept company with them? All the time? She recalls his soft mouth, she tries to think how he had looked at the girl, or whether he had looked around him and eyed young men as well as the girl. But she can't remember that, although she has a very clear image of the girl herself, at least half Alberto's and her age, and very pretty. She was also slightly intellectual in her appearance with that superior bred-in-the-bone look which she knew appealed to Alberto (she was thinking of Rosemary). She had felt a passing stab of self-pity at the time, followed by relief that it was the girl and not she who would have to deal with Alberto later in the evening.

'I'm sure he isn't homosexual,' she tells Dr Gilroy finally.

'Well, we'd better take a look, hadn't we?' He indicates the table with its neatly folded rug at the end. 'Everything off from below the waist.'

How many times has she performed this ritual? All of her life she seems to have been climbing onto doctors' tables and submitting to these body searches. First to have diaphragms fitted, then to have her pregnancies checked, and afterwards the six-weekly check-up to make way for Philip again (though they joked about it, as if it were of no account, the long wait while the baby screamed its head off at nights, and Philip walked the floor. I need something to put me back to sleep, he would say, that would be a help; and her wanting to, but afraid because she was also tired, and putting off the check-up), and then, later, the cervical smear tests, and the one that had looked suspicious but had turned out to be nothing, and the examinations for a dis-lodged uterus, followed by the poking and prodding to decide whether or not she needed a hysterectomy. 'Who needs a worn-out uterus?' the gynaecologist had said. 'I do, it's mine,' she muttered. 'They look like old hot waterbottles,' he'd responded, but he let keep her keep hers all the same), oh the list was endless. They all ended up in the same place though, these examinations, on the table.

And now here she is on another table being examined for venereal disease.

Dr Gilroy's face shines when he has finished his examination. 'You've got a beautiful cervix,' he says. 'It's really very nice.'

She looks at him, shocked. And even though he is a doctor, he appears to blush. He has paid her a compliment which for a moment she has misunderstood.

'I mean, it's very healthy,' he says firmly, and in his most clinical tones. Yet she is touched. He has meant to be kind, and indeed, she senses that in his own way, he has been trying to tell her that he believes her to be above the disgrace of her present situation.

He takes blood from her arm, several samples of it, for a number of different tests, as he explains to her. She cannot bear to watch the process of extraction, the needle lying in her arm, but she glances surreptitiously at the accumulation of phials with her dull dark blood gleaming in the discreet lighting of the consulting room.

'You must have worked very hard in your profession,' he says, as he labels another one. 'To have achieved your position.' She nods.

'I admire the job you do. It can't be easy these days.'

'There are problems in teaching,' she admits. What can she say? She cannot speak of promiscuity or truancy or the perils which beset students. She is no better herself.

As if reading her thoughts, he says, 'I think I will call you something else besides your real name on the laboratory sheet. I don't usually do that, but you may have past pupils there. It would be better. Shall we call you, let's see, what is your second name, yes Mary, Mary Gray?'

'Thank you.' Her eyes fill with tears. It is something she has thought of herself, but has not dared to ask for such consideration.

'I'm quite certain that you don't have any disease, Mary Gray,' he is saying. 'Of course I can't confirm that until I've got the results of these tests back, but I wouldn't give you false hope unless I was sure of what I was saying. I don't believe you have anything to worry about.'

Cushla is speechless, unable to voice her thanks any further, as she stumbles towards the door. 'Why did you leave it so long?' he says, when her hand is reaching for the door handle, only his is there before hers, opening it for her.

'I was so frightened. You wouldn't believe . . .'

'You're too hard on yourself,' he says, and the door closes quietly behind her.

In the street she makes her way to the park, which is full of corrugated concrete waterfalls and small shrubs. Rims of curved perspex surround its perimeter. It is not like a real park at all, but there is afternoon sun and a place to sit amongst other people, each sitting separate from the other, but pushed together anyway, in some contemplation of their condition. Of being alive.

Cushla thinks of Dr Gilroy and his kindness. How might they have looked at one another in some other place, over a dinner table perhaps, or meeting casually on a beach holiday? She is shocked anew. Dr Gilroy is the last person in the world she ever wishes to meet again, let alone socially.

And she is dismayed by some other recognition of herself. What she should be sitting there thinking is that she will never, in all her life, stray from the path of virtue again. That she will be forever unswerving in her fidelities and upright within her conscience. For that is what she has promised herself should she receive good news on her visit to the doctor, and that is what she has been given.

But there are no guarantees, and she knows that it is neither the disastrousness of ageing nor the good office she holds that will save her from herself. Alberto has been an incident, better forgotten, but even he has spoken of love. What if love, in one of its many disguises, were to persuade her again?

A young man, sitting on the bench opposite, smiles at her. He is fresh-faced, an ordinary and vulnerable-looking young man, who flinches when she averts her eyes. She supposes that the best she can hope for is to be preserved by fear.

But sun, and the smile, have warmed her, in spite of herself. The afternoon feels like the end of winter. If she cannot forgive herself, she thinks, who else can she ask to do it for her?

Earthly Shadows

'What sort of an of is that?' The tone is ominous. 'It's existential,' says Jimmy O'Flaherty in a miserable kind of way. 'Or a Wallace Stevens kind of an of. A because of kind of an of.'

Marlon leans back in his chair and looks around the room. Jimmy's eyes follow his as if inspiration might be lurking, waiting to reveal itself, in one of the corners. He wants to be the first to see it. But it is a plain white box-like office, similar to a hundred or so others in the same building. Two large curling Penguin posters adorn the wall above him, one of Iris Murdoch looking worried, and the other of Paul Theroux bearing an odd resemblance in this pose, to an unlamented Minister of Education in the last Government. On the window sill a poinsettia with yellowing leaves struggles to survive in a pot.

The producer seems in no hurry to further their brief acquaintance. He reaches out to pick an imaginary thread from his jeans then turns over a sheaf of pages on his desk with the sort of care that suggests there might be something nasty stuck between the pages. Marlon is a small sandy complexioned man with a crew cut. He wears a green striped shirt with a pink scarf around his neck, and beneath denim-clad legs his feet stick out, encased in pink, green and orange diamond-patterned socks and twinkling red shoes. Born plain Norman Jones, he changed his name to Marlon when he discovered, as he says with a reflective smile, that he was just a raging old queen. Though once darlings I was young, he is likely to add, not that he expects to be believed. It is clear, his manner suggests, that he has always been exactly and charmingly the same, and that with luck he will remain so.

Now he rests his gaze on each of the other four people in the room, returning at last to Jimmy O'Flaherty, the hapless playwright. 'Radio is an exacting art,' he says. 'Yet here before us, we have a play entitled *The Shadow of the Earth*. How, my pet, can there be a shadow *of* the earth. There are shadows of trees, there are shadows of houses, there are shadows of us poor mortal human beings, but earth is an ongoing flowing continuity, is it not, that cannot in itself cast shadows. Am I not correct, Fenella?'

He turns to a large woman who sits far down in her chair opposite him. Her eyes glitter. Her face shines like a hand-painted dinner plate. She loves script conferences. She loves young men who sit like plucked hens in front of her.

'Gross, darling, yes it does sound a little gross,' she says to Marlon. 'Of course,' she says, addressing Jimmy, 'you must take no notice of me, I have really no part in this at all.' Fenella comes from that long and honourable tradition of women whose fiancés were killed in the war and have kept broadcasting running ever since from the bowels of control rooms, where their shadows have fallen further over the hierarchy than Jimmy's earth could ever do. She is also the one person in the world, or broadcasting at least, who remembers Marlon when he was Norman.

'Are you a producer too?' asks Jimmy, for although they have been introduced, her role in the discussion is so far unclear.

'Fenella will present the panel discussion that follows the play, straight after it goes to air. Fen is the Voice.'

'You mean you're going to do it?' says Jimmy, who until this moment has been sure that his play is about to be rejected. He sits very still as if sudden movement might jolt the atmosphere. He has prepared so carefully for this interview, on the face of it could almost rival Marlon himself. He wears a French blue waistcoat under a worn salmon-coloured smoking jacket and he too wears a scarf, a plaid one which hangs all the way to his handmade leather belt with its silver studs. But the hands which hang between his knees are thick and chafed, and he has a slight rough cough, which might be from working on building sites in the cold (he has opted lately for real life experience as part of his apprenticeship for becoming a writer) or from too much smoking. His hand strays to his pocket now, hesitates over his cigarette pack, and drops. He tries to catch Georgie's eyes. She sits with one leg hanging over the padded vinyl arm of her swivel chair, and appears not to see him. He bites a freckled lip. He thinks she is responsible for him, yet she seems to be doing nothing. He could almost swear she was ignoring him.

'If we do it,' Marlon corrects himself gently.

Another voice speaks.

'Hills have shadows. Cliffs have shadows. They're earth. That what you mean, eh lad?'

Jimmy O'Flaherty turns his raw Irish face full of Catholic guilt about deceit and honesty, or whether to tell the truth or not, and blurts out no, before he can stop himself, and realises too late that he may lose an ally in the other corner. Though it is the first time he has had a chance to take a proper look at Brian, who he recalls is a talks producer. Presumably in charge of Fenella's department.

'Oh take no notice of him,' calls Fenella as if they were across a ballroom from each other, 'he adores playing devil's advocate, don't you, darling?'

With relief, Jimmy senses that it is not all bad news if he has, indeed, lost Brian. There is a silence which he suspects he is intended to fill. He flicks a glance towards Georgie May, looking for a cue. She is inspecting a scrag of fingernail.

'Georgie May or may not,' Marlon had said with a leer in his voice when he had invited Jimmy to come in and talk about the script. 'Like it,' he had added. 'She says it's interesting.'

'I'll be awfully grateful for a chat,' Jimmy had said.

'Can't promise a thing, dear heart, but we must follow our script editor's advice.' He was referring to Georgie.

'Don't you like it then?' Jimmy had asked, and known straight away that it was a bad question.

'Lovie, I haven't had an inch of time to actually *read* it,' Marlon said, 'but of course we do produce the odd little play now and then, despite the budget, and we do like to talk to the talent. You know how it is? So we can get acquainted. You do follow me? Well of course you do. Georgie says you're talent, and well frankly, my angel, there isn't much around at the moment, so when I've got a moment I'll have a peek at the script and we can talk about it when I see you. Hnnn?'

'Hnnn,' Jimmy had replied, and hung up on the silence when nothing more happened.

Now, it appears that he is deserted. While Georgie picks her fingernail, Brian takes off one of his roman sandals and unravels a sock from over his foot. He puts his heel up on the desk and takes a large pair of scissors from out of his lower drawer. It is time for him to attack his nails too. The scissors clunk together like hedge clippers.

'It's about the earth's influence over us,' Jimmy says. 'How we're prisoners to the land.'

Brian bangs his scissors on the desk. 'Oh. That. You Kiwis, you're always on about that, aren't you. The land. I am the salt of the earth blah blah blah. You should come from where I do. We don't have quarter-acre sections, and privilege. You think you haven't got class here, but you're all landed gentry. Some of you just have more of it than others.'

'Ee by goom, and I haven't got anything, oh God, oh poor me, oh Brian, why do I have to come to your office, I ask myself a thousand times.' Marlon clutches his head. 'And put that thing away, that foot, that misshapen toe, it's like a dog with its cock out for Chrissake.'

'I'll show you cock.' Brian throws the scissors down and jumps to his feet, his eyes bulging and a thick vein rising in the side of his throat.

'Oh Brian, you couldn't,' says Georgie, speaking at last.

Brian lays his hand on the scissors again.

We're for it now, thinks Jimmy, half rising to disarm him.

'Such angst,' says Fenella. 'Do sit down, Brian, and tell the boy what line the panel will be taking.'

Brian is calmer but does not sit down, as if to prove that he is in charge. He walks up and down the side of the room, tugging savagely at his pointed black beard. He limps slightly in his one bare foot.

'But he cannot tell us what his play is about.' He jabs a thumb in Jimmy's direction.

'Tell us what the play is about, cherub.' Fenella yawns elaborately and in the space between them Jimmy catches a whiff of something rank, like onions. Or gin for breakfast.

'Oh surely not.' Marlon crosses his knees and swings away from them holding his head on one side. 'We don't have to go into all that. Please, not what it is *about*.'

Jimmy stops himself, just in time, from asking Marlon again whether he dislikes the play.

'I really like the old man in it,' says Fenella, compromising by talking about it herself. 'The one who wants to keep the land. It's about a family who're going to lose their farm,' she comments to no one in particular.

Marlon gives an exaggerated squirm. 'Yes, we know, heart, we know.'

'Well the old man is adorable.'

'But it is not about the old man,' cries Jimmy.

Fenella beams triumph. 'They'll always start talking sooner or later. I knew you'd tell me,' she says to Jimmy. She leans over and pats his knee. 'Everyone tells me things. Just pour it all out to little old me.' She adopts a listening pose, hand under her chin, head at a girlish angle.

'It's about the woman. She's the strong one. The one who runs the farm and finishes up saving it.'

'Oh dear. Oh dear me. Not feminism?'

'Well, it's based on feminist thinking.'

'My dear boy, you'll have to play that woman down, she's not a good role model for mothers. I mean, she has got a child, hasn't she?'

'But I would have thought. I mean you're a woman.' Although it is Georgie May whom Jimmy looks at, rather than Fenella. Georgie stares into middle distance, her eyes appear unfocused.

Brian has stopped his pacing and stands in front of Fenella, beaming down at her, his fly a few inches away from her nose. She swallows in a perceptible way.

'I sometimes forget what a sensible woman you are,' he says, rocking backwards and forwards on the balls of his feet. Jimmy notices that the bare one is covered with varicose veins. 'A woman's place is in the home.'

'Oh well, Brian,' Fenella remonstrates, wheeling her chair towards the wall. He follows her. 'That's not quite. Not quite what I meant.' Her voice is faint.

'No no. No, no. Married women. Married women.' He picks up a ruler from the desk and whips it backwards and forwards through the air. Fenella ducks.

'On their backs,' says Georgie.

Brian closes his eyes for a moment, walks to the window, stares out, clenching his fingers around the ruler as if it were Georgie's throat.

'He has had an unfortunate experience,' remarks Georgie, addressing Jimmy. 'I'm sure he'll tell you about it sometime when you have a few hours to spare.' She bites the worrisome fingernail. Her teeth are exact and white, maybe a trifle large.

'It is not my fault that I have never married,' Fenella is saying with deep careful enunciation. 'You can only love once. Deep in your heart. What a lot of unhappiness the world would be spared if more people understood that.'

'She's a strong caring woman,' cries Jimmy. Everyone in the room, except Georgie, stares at him in a perplexed way. 'The woman in the play.' He feels the interview slipping from his grasp. 'Like — like you, Fenella,' he says, inspired with great daring.

'Oh?'

'Like you would be if you had children. I mean, if you *were* married.'

Fenella picks up her purse. 'I can see I'm not needed here.'

'Oh heart,' says Marlon. His voice is tired. 'Do sit down. All this noise, I simply have such a raging headache.' He gestures to Jimmy, pushes himself across the floor on the rollers of his chair, and for a moment Jimmy thinks he will take his hand. 'I went to the pub last night and met an absolutely divine dancer. We won a competition. I won a bottle of brandy, wasn't that clever? Did I tell you I won a bottle of brandy?' He purses his lips and blows a kiss towards Fenella. She has subsided back into her chair, takes out a mirror and pats her nose vigorously with a powder puff as if the morning has already left its traces.

'Now look,' Marlon says in a reasonable way. 'We seem to be talking around in circles. Fenella says the play is about a man and you say it's about a woman?'

'It's about both. But the woman is a strong autonomous character who is a focal point to everyone in the play.'

'But that is a matter of perspective?'

We are getting somewhere, thinks Jimmy. His spirits begin to rise, and he and Marlon smile at each other.

'Surely it is ideologically unsound for a man to be writing about a woman as a central character?' says Brian.

'Exactly, Brian,' says Fenella. 'Personally I would have thought that was one of the first things that would have occurred to *you*, Georgie.'

'But you don't believe in feminism,' says Jimmy.

'Of course I don't, but we live in a world of political realities.'

'Rule Number One. Look after yourself first, second and last,' says Georgie. It looks as if she is about to be drawn.

But the phone is ringing. Georgie picks it up, and answers with her name. The call is for her, she listens intently, swings her chair away into her corner of the room.

'On the other hand,' says Brian, 'it is a perfect vehicle for a panel discussion on the sociological implications of land tenure through acquired wealth versus inheritance.'

'True, true. A consideration,' murmurs Fenella.

'The *nouveau riche* versus the squattocracy. Is there anything to choose between the two?'

'Oh dear.' Marvin looks pained again.

'It's a local issue, of course,' Fenella says. 'Leave it to me to handle.'

'Or, will the poor ever get rich,' cries Brian, ignoring her, and full of sudden enthusiasm.

In the corner, Georgie May has begun to cry, and Jimmy can see what a fragile little person she really is, even though she looks so tough and self-assured on the outside, dressed up in her gay tights and sweater, with her black hair falling like straight silk over her ears. She pushes it back and twines it round in her fingers. Her ring finger has a vulnerable white line around it, where a ring has recently been removed. Her tears are silent but they cover her face. Suddenly she leaps to her feet and rushes out of the room.

Fenella raises her eyebrows. 'Sports or newsroom?'

'Probably both together,' says Marlon.

Fenella's ample bosom quivers and she lets out a snort like a tidal wave.

'That's what happens to married women who play around,' says Brian.

'Divorce.' Marlon is watching Jimmy's stricken face. He cannot take his eyes from the doorway where Georgie has disappeared, as if through concentration he might will her reappearance. There is something regretful about the way Marlon looks at Jimmy.

'Well, separated, so far. Unless she sees the light. Your Mrs May has a varied sort of life, Jimmy.' Fenella comments. 'But then you'll know about that.'

'They never do. Learn. Don't want to.' Brian is sinking into late morning depression. 'You see, she'll come out of it all right. They always get the money. Women do. It's a scheme, they have it from the beginning.'

'Brian's been to his men's group again,' says Marlon.

'So have you, haven't you, darling?' Fenella is enamoured of her own wit and snorts again. She glances from her watch to Jimmy and back again. She too has noticed his longing eyes follow Georgie out of the room.

'So you are going to do it?' Jimmy ventures, feeling that a resolution is in order. He knows he should be asking about the fee, and tries to remember what the Writers' Guild has said about contracts — he won't be able to face the meeting on Thursday night if he is not business-like straight away, sees his invitation to join the committee slipping through the cracks.

He takes another deep breath, flexes his thumbs in a pattern like a cross between his knees. 'I'm so glad you like it.'

Marlon looks at him blankly.

Jimmy laces all his fingers, working the palms rapidly backwards and forwards from the wrists, so that he pops out a noise like the awful underarm squelch that boys at primary school make to disgust girls, and blushes. 'The play, I'm so glad you like the play.'

Marlon wrinkles his nose. 'Like it?'

'I thought you did,' Jimmy O'Flaherty murmurs without looking at him. 'It's a very important work to me. Seminal. It's my life.' He puts his hand on his breast, without thinking, without affectation, and is overcome with fresh and deeper embarrassment.

'Darling heart, I'm sure it is. You've a great career in front of you.'

'I do?'

But there is foreboding in the air. Fenella and Marlon have drawn closer together, almost in a physical way, bound by the old unbreakable ties of knowledge, which pass for, might even be friendship, and anticipate the outsider.

'Writing soapies, I think you'll be exquisite.' Marlon lights the cigarette Jimmy so badly needs and feels he has renounced.

'They'll love you in telly,' murmurs Fenella.

'Oh yes, lucky old chap, they will, won't they.' Marlon flicks ash with care and accuracy towards a distant ashtray.

'But.' Jimmy seeks words. He is in love with words. Like Georgie, they have eluded him.

'Sorry, sweetness,' says Fenella, '*Coup de grâce*. Mind-bogglingly crapulous. Terrible shit.' Her vowels are round and delicious, fluid behind her full red mouth. 'We should have brought spoons to eat it with. Really, positively vulgar.'

'All that sentiment. Sheer humanism, I'm afraid. In spite of the of.' Marlon smiles with great warmth at Jimmy.

Jimmy stands up, sure he is going to weep just like Georgie May. 'A misunderstanding. I thought you were going to do it.'

'But we are, ducks,' says Marlon.

'But why?'

'Fills a gap. Hole in the schedule,' says Brian. He has taken a barley sugar which has gone sticky from out of his drawer and is delicately picking staples off it before he puts it in his mouth.

Marlon removes a shred of tobacco from the tip of his tongue. 'You're not taking this personally, are you? Oh dear.' He looks helplessly at Fenella, who shrugs, and sits up straight with her purse on her knees. 'You know, I've no objection to giving people what they want. I don't mind doing crap if it makes them happy.'

'Makes *who* happy?' Jimmy hears the note of pleading in his voice. It is a sound he knows will come back to haunt him.

'The people, angel. They'll love your *Shadows on the Wall*.'

'*Of the Earth*.'

'Oh. Earth. Yes. Of. See how confusing?'

'You ain't gunna do it.'

Fenella rolls her eyes. ' Standards. A university boy too.'

'You're . . . not . . . going . . . to . . . do . . . my . . . play.'

'Bless you, heart, you'll never get on if you don't get on top of all this subjective emotion,' says Marlon. 'It's one thing for the soapies but it'll never do in real life. Of course we're going to do the play. Now run upstairs and tell them to fix you up with a contract. The money's lovely, pet, it's just gone up again.'

There is a rushing in Jimmy's ears. Far below, he hears the sound of traffic. 'Thank you,' he says.

'I've just remembered,' says Brian, when Jimmy reaches the door.

'Well,' Marlon says, 'what a consciousness-raising morning. Treat us to your memories, Brian.'

'What about the Maoris?'

'Maoris? What about the Maoris?'

'There aren't any. In the script.'

'Oh dear. No. Neither there are.' Marlon rubs his nose.

'We don't have to have them,' says Fenella.

'You ought to,' says Brian. 'With the land, and that.'

'La, look who's talking.' But Marlon is worried. He turns to Jimmy. 'Can you do us a Maori?'

'I guess. I don't know.'

'On the other hand,' Brian's voice is lugubrious, 'maybe he'd better not. Ideologically unsound. From his point of view, that is. They're bound to phone in and complain.'

'But they'll complain if he doesn't.' Marlon pulls his nose in genuine bafflement.

'I could do you an Irishman,' says Jimmy.

'I'll bet. No, let's be devils, we're in the business of taking risks. Make it a Maori, or even a couple if you can manage it, Jimmy my sweet.'

Fenella sighs. 'I can always get rid of them on the panel.'

Jimmy closes the door behind him. Georgie May walks down the corridor towards him, her face composed, if a little pale. There is no trace of tears.

'Well, that went all right, didn't it,' she says brightly.

Jimmy O'Flaherty scowls. His heart is clenched with envy. 'Sports or newsroom?' he asks.

She glances at him. Hesitates. 'Newsroom. I'm going back to my husband, you know.'

143

'Of course,' says Jimmy.

'You didn't let them worry you, did you?' She nods in the direction of the office he has just left.

'Nah.' His fingers curl round the cigarettes.

'You shouldn't, you know. You're a real writer now.' She plants a feathery kiss on his cheek. 'You can take me to lunch when you get your cheque.'

But her step is purposeful as she heads back towards the office.

Jimmy leans on the lift button. He is uncertain whether or not he is supposed to be happy. He waits to be taken away.

The Tennis Player

1

On the leg from Bombay Ellen sat upright beside a cello which had had a seat booked for it because its owner said it was a Stradivarius. The cabin attendants seemed more gracious towards the cello than to the children who had joined the flight at Bombay. The lavatories were jammed with unflushed paper, service came less often than in the early part of the flight, and babies cried. Ellen offered to walk a child whose mother looked like a delicate Asian figurine.

She and the child stood and looked down at Turkey for a long time through the domed glass at the rear of the plane.

'Are you a missionary?' asked a woman across the aisle, when she returned.

Ellen shook her head and smiled politely. She had been travelling for nearly thirty hours. She had begun to think that she would like to be a cello.

2

In London she lugged her huge suitcase up five flights of stairs and found herself in a bedsit under the eaves of a building in Eccleston Square that looked elegant from the outside and was a dump on the inside. There was a fire escape out to the roof just like in *The Girls of Slender Means*.

Only Ellen was forty-five and the war was over.

3

She walked down the street until she came to a Mr Wimpy food bar. She was still unhealthily full of airline food, yet the cardboard-and-onion smell of packaged hamburgers was irresistible. It was like Friday night in Newtown, close to home. The restaurant was full, with black faces and white in about equal proportion, and she was certain that the black faces were friendlier than the white.

Afterwards, she went to the women's lavatory at Victoria Station and queued behind the barrier. The large black woman in charge shouted out, 'Which one of you ladies been and gonna done a wee wee on my floor?' Nobody answered and Ellen knew she thought it was her.

Her cheeks burned. She stepped over the puddle.

4

On the way home (for, for the moment there was no other, except Eccleston Square) she stopped to buy grapes from a fruit barrow, and fumbled with the unfamiliar coins.

'Doesn't know the bleeding time of day, does she?' the man who ran the fruit barrow said to a group of schoolgirls with cheeks like beastly English apples. She gave him money, took what he said was her change, and fled without the grapes. She heard the laughter of the girls as she hurried down the street. Stung, she turned and walked back, shouting at the fruit vendor, *fuck you, fuck you, ah fuck you.*

Then she ran for fear the bobbies would pick her up.

She felt better until she got back to Eccleston Square.

She spoke of herself as an ordinary woman. But she was used to living in a house with restored ceilings and pale walls that faced out to sea. She listened to classical music on the radio when she took her morning baths.

In the room, she sat on the bed and wondered if there would be a nuclear attack before she got back to New Zealand and what were the chances of seeing her family again.

5

The best part of every day was saying *fuck you* to the fruit vendor when she passed. You could almost say they were on nodding terms. In Wellington, the city she came from, she had observed a woman dressed in a yellow and red cloak, who ran from behind a door at the railway station to feed pigeons. This activity was strictly forbidden. She did it when she thought no one was watching. Only someone always was. She got chased by a station attendant with a broom. Ellen could not stop thinking about her.

6

She went to a communion service in Westminster Abbey. It was Mothering Sunday and she began to cry. A woman in a good tweed suit and a slouched hat stood up in the middle of the service when the choir had just finished singing the Twenty-third Psalm. The woman shouted out to the congregation that they were all fools and hypocrites, and mistaken and misled. Ellen wanted to cheer when she was led away across the cold stones. Mostly because it might have been her getting caught but was not. Instead she drank the blood of Christ, and resolved to speak more forthrightly to the fruit vendor.

7

The next day she bought an Israeli avocado and a bottle of German wine at a corner store and took them back to the room. On a roof garden opposite to her, three men carried a garden up from the street, and she saw that it was full of flowering daffodils. In the square below, two men unlocked the gate and went inside to play tennis, locking the gate behind them, so that no one could get in.

It amazed her that nobody shook the bars. Rally, they cried, game love set.

On the day following that, she bought two cobs of bright gold corn. She had never eaten such sweet corn. It made her want to cry again, it tasted so much of home, and childhood, only better.

Outside snow had begun to fall, and the three men had appeared on the rooftop garden to take the daffodils away. She wondered how the corn had ripened in weather like this, and realised that of course it must have been imported. She rummaged through the rubbish tin and found the label on the packaging. The corn had been grown in South Africa.

8

She knew she was as nutty as a peanut slab when she got on the train at Charing Cross to go to Paris, but thought that maybe it wasn't showing. The thing was, she was getting out of it. She opened her phrase book. She had passed School Certificate French. She had meant to refresh herself but hadn't found the time. It felt as if it was thirty years since she had recited a French verb.

It was.

Exactly.

9

She sat for a long time watching the railyards turn to open fields, glimpsed grass and trees through mist. She was so afraid that now she would have been grateful for Eccleston Square. She had been running late and missed the *bureau de change*. Effectively, she was bound for Paris with no money. She passed her hand over her stomach where her travellers' cheques were strapped in her money belt. The belt had worked round and the zip chafed her skin. The lack of money was something to worry about, and she supposed it would preoccupy her all the way to Paris. Her husband would have said, if you haven't got something to worry about, you'll invent something.

Which was all very well.

But if there was no *bureau de change* at the station, how would she get a taxi? She must also go to the lavatory on the train, or the boat, or somewhere, because if she did not, maybe she would have to pay to go at the station in Paris, and then if she had no money, and they would not let her in, how would she take off her money belt to get the travellers' cheques out so she could change them anyway? There was so much to think about. Since she had been away she kept trying to cross things off lists she must do, if she was to survive alone in Europe, but instead she continually remembered more things to add. She did not know how she had ever looked after her children when it was so difficult to look after herself.

She pushed her gloved hand distractedly through her hair and avoided the feet of the young man sitting facing her, as they threatened to become entangled with hers. The feet were clad in fine soft leather boots.

10

She had observed the way people did not stare at each other in England, and the way that they did not make random comments to each other. Even though she had not spoken to anyone except the fruit vendor for several days she knew she should resist the urge to speak.

11

The young man pretended to be asleep whenever she looked at him. She knew he pretended by the way he moved his feet. He had started being tidy with them.

After a while he pretended to wake up and took out a book. She saw that it was a collection of Andrew Marvell's poems. She felt ashamed that she was only reading a novel, even though it was by Barbara Pym who was now rediscovered.

The young man wore designer jeans. He picked one of his feet up off the floor and placed it on the seat so that his very long leg was cocked along it, and his shapely crotch exposed towards her.

It was as good as a smile.

'Are you a student?' she said, looking at his book, and recalling English I.

'No,' he said, but he did smile. He had strong white teeth, and his face was lean and tanned. He turned the book a little so that she could appreciate the cover. 'It's a good read.'

'Have you been to Paris before?' she blurted.

'Not since last week,' he said.

He pointed to the luggage compartment. She saw then, two tennis racquets in frames. They looked shiny and expensive.

'I'm a tennis player. I play in tournaments. Most weeks I play somewhere in Europe. This week and last, it's been Paris.'

'How exciting,' she said, and heard herself breathless and a little tremulous. 'Are you famous? Should I know you? I'm from New Zealand, you see, we don't see all the games, well only the finals at Wimbledon, I might not have seen, you understand . . . ?'

'No, not so exciting, no truly. Of course, in New Zealand I can see you might not have . . . sometimes on television, yes, but in New Zealand, well I can understand that. I do win some.'

He smiled again. She recognised false modesty when she saw it.

12

He was kind though, generous with details. They told each other the story of their lives, listening carefully to one another. He came from Devon. His parents had thought he might do better than be a tennis player but he didn't understand their problem. It was a good job. It took a long time to tell her this. She, having had a longer life, took even more time.

They hurtled past fields she could barely see because the mist now hugged the edge of the railway tracks like white fur.

They discussed the agrarian patterns of Great Britain. In the fifth form, she had been taught about grain production in East Anglia. She could not understand its relevance to her life. She had wondered if, coming here to England for the first time, she would discover why it was important to her to learn about its grainfields when she had only a rough idea of where wheat was grown in New Zealand.

His tone was almost sharp. 'Of course it's important,' he said. 'It is a central factor in the British economy.' He paused, frowned. 'And New Zealand depends on Britain, doesn't it?'

How curious, she thought, if, after all, an ear or two of wheat were to come between her and the consummation of what was clearly shaping up to be the most classic interlude in her life. A young man, in Paris, where despite the portents on this side of the Channel, it was officially spring and bound to be fine. A small subterranean voice begged her to remind herself that it was simply fucking in a general sort of way that she had in mind, rather than with this particular young man. She dismissed the voice. For the moment, she thought that if her husband were here, right at this minute, she would probably prefer the tennis player.

'Would you ever play in South Africa?' she asked him, holding her breath.

'Never,' he said with fervour. She breathed a long sigh of relief, forgiving him East Anglia. She saw his head on the pillow beside hers, and the index finger of her right hand sitting inside its new glove, purchased in Oxford Street the day before, traced his profile in her mind's eye. She knew already that she was bound never to forget him.

'In the mornings we eat breakfast outside at the sidewalk cafés. You must do that,' he was saying. 'It is the only way to have breakfast in Paris.'

13

At Dover she thought the white cliffs were a hill covered with birdshit. They had disappeared behind the hovercraft before she had time to appreciate them.

'Is that all?' she said to him. 'Is that all?'

At the terminal people had turned to look at them. He had bought her coffee and croissants, and refused to allow her to pay. 'In New Zealand,' he said. Already it had been decided that he must play the New Zealand circuit some summer soon.

She felt herself walking with the special pride of someone who has recently become one half of a new couple. It occurred to her that he might be very well known indeed. Look at him, she imagined the eyes that followed them were saying, he has a new woman. Perhaps it would get into the papers. Young tennis player woos mystery woman. Antipodean sweetheart — how long can this romance last? In praise, again, of older women.

'You'll be speaking French in a minute,' he said, and too late she realised that the English Channel was behind her.

She opened her phrase book at Arrivals and Departures. 'I have two hundred cigarettes, some wine and a bottle of spirits,' she said, frivolous in her mood.

'The children are on my wife's passport,' he said, running his finger down the list.

She laughed out loud. '*Non. Je ne suis que de passage.*'

He nodded approvingly. 'Passing through, eh? *Bon.*' He opened his hands, a mock Gallic gesture. '*Je n'ai rien à déclarer aussi.*'

He put his hand on her phrasebook. 'Don't worry about it so much.'

14

The train stopped often in the French countryside. The small towns all seemed to have rubbish tips for backyards. Their conversation became erratic. It was still raining.

'You must be privileged if you play tennis in England,' she mused, and aware already that he was. But she had been thinking of Eccleston Square.

His head was slipping sideways towards her shoulder. She could smell him. He smelled like a new racquet, gutsy and clean.

'Probably. Tell me some more about New Zealand,' he said drowsily, without minding whether she did or not. She watched him. She thought of something special she would do for him.

15

The lock in the bedroom door worked by a number of turns in either direction. She could not work out the sequence. Not only could she not get in, but once in she could not get out either. She had to call reception three times before she had mastered it, and on the last occasion she was near to hysteria. The young man on the desk came upstairs on his own to explain it to her the first two times. His English was bad. The third time he brought another man, who spoke good English. He explained the lock in a slow and patient way as if she were simple. She considered leaving the hotel and going to another, but night had fallen and she did not know where to go.

When it seemed as if she understood the mechanism of the lock she sat in the room and shook. Several hours had passed since the tennis player had last bought her food, and the hotel had no restaurant. Even it it had, she was afraid to leave the room.

Still, at least she liked it. After Eccleston Square it was like a return to some other life where ease and comfort were again possible. The king-sized bed was covered with a frilled quilt with a pattern of pink and green peacocks, and there were rose-coloured lights on the wall. There were gold-coloured taps in the bathroom and a deep bath.

The louvre doors led out onto a wrought iron balcony over-looking Rue Pasquier. The life of the city stretched below her had she chosen to walk out onto the balcony, though for the moment the sound of traffic had caused her to close the doors so that she could hear herself think.

She knew she would not sleep if she did not eat, and maybe drink as well, and that the longer she left it the more difficult it would be to set out.

Carefully she tried the lock and this time the combination worked to perfection. Emboldened, she left the hotel and walked quickly along the boulevard in the direction of St Augustin. Her handbag was comfortably full of francs. 'You'll be all right now, won't you?' he had said when he left her at the counter of the *bureau de change*. 'I'm sorry I can't see you to a taxi.' He had become tense and athletic, fretting with his tennis racquets. He had explained on the first train, in England, that his game was on the other side of Paris. As it was, he would be cutting things fine to get there on time.

Traffic swirled past her. She could not see where the centre line of the road was, or indeed, if there were any true sides to the roads, as a car mounted the pavement and ran its left-hand tyres alongside her ankles. She leapt out of its path and watched it subside into the path of an oncoming car, which swerved in its turn.

Right up until the last moment she knew that she had been shamefully hoping. Even in the taxi, re-counting her money, which she had been short-changed the first time it was given to her, and she had had to demand in a loud high voice that it be counted again, she wondered if he had heard her tell him the name of the hotel, and regretted that she had not had the courage to repeat it when he was leaving.

It was after the second time that the lock on the door would not open that she admitted his expression. It was, she remembered, decent and perfectly nice, marred by a slight but growing sense of impatience.

She found a restaurant. The waiter was young. He did not speak any English at all. She pointed out a phrase in her small blue book. *Je ne parle pas bien le français. Je viens de Nouvelle Zélande.* He brought her a carafe of wine without being asked. When she drank it thirstily he brought her another, and indicated to her what he had decided it would be best for her to eat.

Vous êtes très aimable, she wrote on her paper napkin when she left. She felt undone by such simple kindness.

Like the kindness of the tennis player. They had not talked about his aunts, but she knew without such a conversation taking place, that he was kind to them. He would be good to them if they were ever foolish enough to go to Paris alone. He might even try to dissuade them from going.

16

Inside the room she felt free, with a sudden odd delight that she was alone. She leaned against the door with her back to it. It was April, and she was in Paris. She had come from the other side of the world for this. She had transacted money. She knew the combination of her lock. She had bought a meal. In a minute or so she would run a large hot bath.

She had not drawn the curtains yet, and outside the night sky shone with reflected light.

Ellen walked to the doors leading out onto the balcony and opened them, breathing deeply and calmly. She stepped outside, and a fine rain was falling. She gripped the edge of the wrought iron balcony, and was happy.

As she stood there, a curious thing happened. The astonishing traffic began to grind to a halt beneath her. Two cars hit each other with a sickening thud. The drivers leapt out of the cars, and without looking at each other, raised their fists in her direction, as if it was she who was responsible for their misfortune.

More cars began to stop. Within moments Rue Pasquier was clogged with cars askew where their owners had abandoned them with their motors running. Behind the cars that had stopped, drivers in the oncoming wave who could not see what was happening began to sound their horns.

Ellen was increasingly bewildered by the commotion. But it was surely a phenomenon which, if studied, must give insight and meaning to the character of the French. She prided herself in a lively curiosity. The men who had first waved their fists at her were now shouting at each other. But other drivers, less hapless, still appeared transfixed by something at the point where she stood. She thought that it must be above her and looked upwards, putting her hand on the wall over her head.

A man headed towards the balcony then, laughing and shouting at the same time. She drew back, afraid. She was not so far above the street that a man could not scale the wall to where she stood.

She caught a word. She was sure it was not in her phrase book.

But she understood.

17

When the door to the balcony was double locked behind her she ran her bath. She took off all her clothes. She looked at herself in the steamed-up glass.

The wife who might pass for a maiden aunt or a missionary who might pass for a whore looked back though it was difficult to say whether she looked any more like one of these than the other.

Most likely, she thought, she resembled the cello.

The Sugar Club

She was having dinner at The Sugar Club. The walls were bleak, the tables bare, and the bentwood chairs reminded her of an earlier home than the one she lived in now. The music crunched like gravel underfoot. She was dining with clever women. The food was excellent. They drank expensive wine.

At the table next to them an actor and an actress who were said to be in love and were both well known stared at each other with stony faces. They ate their meal quickly and left.

She stood up and walked through the restaurant and out the door marked Toilets. There was a passage beyond painted brick red. At the end of the passage there was the promised lavatory. There was a bowl of daffodils on the cistern. The floor was painted turquoise blue.

When she came out of the lavatory again she was confused in the brick red passage. She couldn't see the door through which she had come from the restaurant. The passage ahead ended in an alleyway that opened directly onto the street. A bicycle stood propped against the wall at the end of the alleyway. A gust of stars appeared to pass in the distant sky above the bicycle. She thought of riding the bicycle away into the night but she knew she would fall off it. Not just tonight, but any night. She had been able to freewheel once but it was a long time ago.

She opened the only door that she could see. It opened into the kitchen. It was completely white and three chefs wearing hats were sitting down talking. They looked frightened and disturbed by her entrance.

A fourth person stood with her back to the door and did not see her. It was a woman, judging by the voice, for she sang a sweet thin tune.

'. . . She wears red feathers and a hooley hooley skirt . . .' sang the woman.

She retreated without closing the door. It was banged shut behind her.

Feeling foolish now, in the alleyway, she looked for a way to escape. Beside her, merging with the brick red paint, she saw the outline of a door. She tried it and it opened to reveal the interior of The Sugar Club.

She walked through the restaurant with her usual air of assurance. At the table she sat down with the clever women who were pleased to see her return.

'Oh God,' she said, leaning her head on her hand for a moment. 'Oh sugar.'

Bloody sugar.

'Oh bloody sugar,' she said.

Pudding

From time to time I need to go away in order to write in peace. This is not to say that I am not surrounded by a great deal of peace of other people's making. People, meaning family and friends, have great respect for my need for peace and quiet these days. 'Ellen is working,' they say to each other, 'she must be left in peace.' I am grateful and sometimes overwhelmed by this consideration. So overwhelmed that I have to go away.

I go to a variety of places, but most particularly to a motel a long way from where I live. I think it is best if I do not tell you where the motel is, for the motel-keeper's wife figures slightly in this story, and I do not think she would appreciate being identified. Her role is not significant, in that it could be filled by another person, and I have thought of cutting her out altogether, but I find that difficult, simply because she was there. Instead, I will tell you that the motel is perched on the edge of sand dunes on one of those bays that stretch limitlessly around the eastern coast of the north of New Zealand, the sand so blazingly white by day, that it makes the eyes reel in their sockets when you look at it, and in the moonlight makes you think of Peter O'Toole playing Lawrence of Arabia. Which leads one on to thinking about going to the movies and sitting in the back stalls of picture theatres of which there are, or were, countless replicas of each other, in every little town that anyone has ever lived in in this country of ours, in the days before we all had television. Oh, if you want to be exact, some had television when O'Toole played Lawrence. Like I said, not all of us.

I was thinking especially along these lines when I went to this motel to write a film script. I had taken a copy of William Goldman's *Adventures in the Screen Trade* with me, and my portable electronic typewriter, a tin of lambs' tongues in jelly, which I find a delicacy of unparalleled delight, a number of avocados, and several bottles of wine cooler. Everything was in its place, and I had already been in residence for three days. On the night of which I write, I had spent a great deal of time walking up and down the beach *thinking visually*. It was mid-week and the motel was almost empty, even though it was early summer. Sensibly, I had come just before the school holidays. Next week it would be different. For now, I had the motel, built to simulate a

Spanish hacienda, more or less to myself. The beach to myself. My splendid panoramic thoughts all to myself. To tell the truth, it could get a little boring; I often long, in these periods of controlled peacefulness, for the phone, to which nobody except my nearest relatives has access to the number, to be rung in case of emergency, to ring (well, hardly anyone, my agent always rings long distance, it pleases him that I have so much discipline) or that it be time to decently call it a day and turn on television.

Hence the hours between late afternoon, when it feels as if I should be at home preparing a meal, and the time when it is dark can be difficult to navigate. I walk along the beach then, watching with a certain wonder the growing accumulation of footprints which turn outwards at the toes, threading backwards and forwards along the sand, tracing and retracing the way they have come; these splay-footed feet wearing sneakers are my feet.

It is relevant here to give a little of the layout of this motel and its surroundings. The setting is a lonely landscape with only two or three houses to be seen in the far distance. They are of the very large cedarwood variety, and their owners are rarely seen, if indeed they are in them at all. These brooding livery-looking houses may well be the cottages of the rich for all I know.

The motel units run parallel to the beach, separated from the sand by a narrow strip of kikuyu grass and then a band of very tall grass which is quite impenetrable. You would cut yourself on the whiplike grass if you were to attempt to walk through it. The only route from the motel to the sea, then, is down a narrow track in the dunes at the far end of the units. If one stays in any but the end unit it is necessary to pass the windows of all the other units in the row in order to reach the track. The windows are all floor-to-ceiling-length glass. Essential of course; the view is magnificent. As they say in the guidebooks. Straight out from the window of my unit (I always have the same one, its window is angled best for morning light where I have my typewriter) there is a barbecue area. I have never seen anyone using it, but then, as I said, I do not come in the season.

That is the time and the location. Add to this, the cast. So far, there is only me, and a suggestion, as you will have noted, that the motel-keeper's wife is to have a walk-on part. There is also about to be a guest appearance by a thin woman of indeterminate years and pale grey hair. She arrived at lunchtime, driving a sedate and well-cared-for Austin, gleaming with old polish. She struck me as the kind of woman who would not buy a Japanese car on principle. I, unfortunately, am the kind of woman who cannot afford to have principles. Not in this business anyway.

I had seen the thin woman sitting in a deck chair on the balcony of the unit at the farthest end away from the track. Twice she had got up and picked her way past my window, but when she came to the track it seemed to intimidate her. She looked round furtively to see whether I was watching this failure of nerve, and when she observed that I had my head down and wasn't looking, or at least, that I wasn't going to show that I was looking, she returned the way she had come, passing close by me, her head shaded by a large sunhat tied in place by a scarf knotted under her chin, and her hands encased in fingerless gloves made of white muslin. I thought of giving her a fright and saying hullo, but that seemed silly, like breaking the rules on the beach at Brighton. For I suspected her of Englishness. Or an escapee from the Raj. Oh the far, the far far pavilions.

By five o'clock she had given up all pretence of going to the beach and was sitting quietly in her deck chair. She looked pensive and refined.

Another carload of people arrived, and this car told me a great deal about the people who rode in it, a sharp white Cordia Turbo. Middle-range young executive, I thought. Or a computer salesman (maybe both). Doing well anyway. Consumer goodies. If I were putting a young upwardly mobile executive and his wife in my film I would appoint them a Cordia Turbo. Unfortunately this was not possible. My film was to be period history.

Having, as I thought, summed up the man and the woman in the car, and suspecting momentarily that they might not be married to each other, I did not think much more about them. I was restless and it was time to go to the beach again.

I walked for a long time. I wanted to get away from the motel for it was beginning to feel crowded. I realised that I had been short-changing the virtue of solitude. I didn't have the beach to myself either. Several people passed me, and then a boy on a trail-bike. In the distance there was a truck parked on the sand, and a man and a woman and a child were gathering driftwood and stacking it on the back of the truck. I could see that they looked poor, and the woman wore a scarf knotted under her chin, though not in the manner of the pensive English woman. Rather like a peasant in jeans. This was a new scenario, and as set pieces went, quite perfect in its way. Vintage Bergman.

As I came back level with the motel, I saw that the couple whom I identified as the pair in the Cordia Turbo had come down to the beach. The man had taken off his tie, and was swinging the jacket of his three-piece suit in one hand. He was a heavily built man, perhaps in his forties, certainly older than his companion, a woman whom I took to be thirty or so. She had taken off her high-heeled sandals, and was drawing a pattern in the sand with one varnished little toe. Her legs were the colour of pale buffed teak, shown off to good advantage by a white linen suit. If she was fractionally plump it was not to her discredit, for everything about her shone with health and an attention to the details of her appearance. I could not help but admire her, and the tilt of her head as she looked up at her companion and smiled at him, with all her bright white teeth surrounded by a glossy smile. Still, they looked awkward on the sand, in their expensive clothing, and I saw them turn back to the motel. Relieved, I decided to wait a few minutes until they were back inside. I had noted that they were in the end unit, facing the track. Soon I too would go inside and eat the food out of the tins, and expensive fruit, have a drink, ring home, and prepare to listen to the sea all night long. For I find it hard to sleep when I am at the beach.

The sun was dropping over the sea. If you looked out over the water it was blinding, but the air was still tremendously yellow and bright. I made my way towards the motel. When I was half way across the grass I stopped, embarrassed.

There, in front of the window of the end unit, was a man bending over with his back towards me. I thought he was taking off his socks. He had taken off everything else. I was confronted by what, in our vulgar New Zealand way, we describe as a brown-eye.

I would agree, if it were suggested to me, that my imagination was overheated, but I swear, at that moment, the man's arsehole looked as big as a saucer. I looked away, afraid that he would stand up and catch me looking. Anyone can get caught with their pants down. So I have often heard it said. But something about the way he moved drew my eye back again.

The man was not taking off his socks at all. He was bending over the woman in white who was lying on the end of the bed. The polished brown legs flicked up around his waist, and I caught, out of the corner of my eye, the action of a deep diver taking the plunge.

Again, I have to admit to a certain admiration for their style.

I moved around inside my unit with exaggerated care. I found that my hands were shaking. I felt a deep consternation for the couple from the Cordia Turbo. How desperate they must have been to make love that they had not pulled the curtains, I thought. How terrible they will feel if they look out and find someone peering in.

Of course there is no one to peer in at them except me, I told myself. The people on the beach do not come up here. The motel-keeper and his wife will not look; they are used to such impatience, hands which shake when they sign the register, such a surfeit of civility and normalcy from people who will pay with cash instead of cheques or credit cards in the morning; they have been trained to look the other way. And the woman from the Raj will have already locked her door and hidden the key even from herself.

So why should I, so full of concern and love for them, (for overwhelming passion is attractive, you must admit, it is the stuff of movies after all) be so undone?

I opened a tin of meat, and cut open some tomatoes. Ritual-istically, I set the table. But I was not hungry. I opened a wine cooler. When I am at the beach it is my habit to sit on the bal-cony and drink something light, and watch the setting sun. Tonight I realised that this was not possible, if the couple did not close their curtains. The balcony looked across to their window and while, in fact, I could not see into their unit from my balcony, they could see me if they looked up and not be cer-tain whether or not they were within my range of vision. I drank some of the wine beverage rather quickly, standing at the sink, looking through the window that faced the back of the motel complex, trying to take pleasure from the assortment of debris I had collected from the beach and the grass outside and placed on the windowsill: half a thrush egg, its turquoise colour like pure light on the dark wood; another piece of eggshell, which I could not identify, white with pale brown speckling and a soft matt finish; a piece of wood with a regular even grain worn smooth; the skeleton of a fish with a stone in its eye; the thrown head of a spinifex; and a handful of goose barnacles.

I cannot stay in here, I thought. The place was driving me crazy. I was certain they must be finished by now. Long enough had elapsed for the act to be completed, certainly given the urgency I had witnessed, and now they must realise that the curtains were open.

Feeling resolute, as if it required a significant act of courage on my part, I walked outside, and back towards the sea. When I came level with the end unit I kept my head down, but with a quick neighbourly concern to ensure that everything was now in order, I flicked my eyes sideways.

The curtains were open.

The brown eye was disappearing in and out of the folds of its own cheeks with increasing rapidity, and the bright petal-pointed toes were twinkling in the air a very considerable distance from each other.

I walked on down to the beach. I felt I was being watched, but dared not look over my shoulder. I sat down on the sand and my heart was pounding. I was gripped by a quite extraordinary agitation, as if I had been caught in some discreditable act. I put my head down on my knees and tried to think. Now that I had come back to the beach I had placed myself in a terrible position.

I was going to have to get back to the unit. I looked at the toetoe grass at the edge of the sand. I had already missed the path and got lost in it once that week and, truly, it had imparted the sense of being lost in a jungle maze. I had no choice but to return by the track. Weighing up everything in my mind, I was seized by a great compassion for these two foolish lovers. They should be told that they were being observed. I would knock on the door, I decided, and stand there waiting for it to open, with downcast eyes, but when one of them opened the door (it would be the man I was sure), I would say, with a slight worldly faraway smile, that they may not have happened to notice, but in fact, their curtains were open. They would be embarrassed but grateful for my discreet and kindly intervention. I braced myself, feeling a trifle breathless, and started to get to my feet. But I sank back down onto the sand with a groan. It wouldn't do, of course.

My concern was replaced by anger. It was a public beach, it was a common access to and from the beach to the unit, there was no other. Why should the utterly egocentric and hedonistic copulation of these two people interfere with my evening? Why shouldn't I look at them fucking?

Ah, this was closer to it. I reminded myself with some severity, that I was not only a scriptwriter but a novelist as well.

It occurred to me in a rush, that as a writer who wrote, from time to time, about the sexuality of others, I may have an obligation to my art. For how often did the critics say, that all sex was the writer's own experience translated into the behaviour of others? As if we were the only peep-show in town. Now, I was being presented with the opportunity to undertake research. I had a duty to observe this couple.

I was very relieved when I came to this conclusion, and now I did stand up, brushing the sand off my trousers and generally preparing myself to work again.

To my astonishment, I saw that the Raj woman was approaching me along the sand. I had not seen her come to the beach, and I tried to remember when this might have occurred. I concluded, in the brief seconds it took me to consider the matter, that it must have been when I had my back to the sea and was contemplating the birds' eggshells on my windowsill. Now she was walking sturdily and purposefully, as if she was about to catch an elephant. She had donned a pair of dark glasses, and she still wore a sunhat, although the sun was starting to slide towards the sea.

Her presence disturbed me, yet I thought, with fortitude, that larger problems than this had conspired in the past to keep me from my job and so I turned towards the path, although this time I did give her a nod for I felt she might be lonely in this vast seascape. She returned the nod, her chin firm and resolute as if she too had tasks to accomplish.

At the crest of the path, facing the motel, I stopped. The room had assumed the proportions of a golden bowl of light. The couple on the bed were lying with their shining limbs entwined in that comfortable and affectionate contemplation of their lovemaking which people assume when it is over. The young woman's fingers caressed her lover's back and earlobes, as if he had given her a very nice time indeed.

I tingled with disappointment. Apparently it was over.

But my attention was drawn away from the window by an odd scratching noise. I looked over to where it was coming from, and saw that the motel-keeper's wife was hoeing the grass around the barbecue area. It seemed to be an odd thing to be doing, at that time of evening. (I am not sure why, it was as good a time as any I suppose, although I knew that it was the time when guests arrived, and besides she had been sitting out in the sun for most of the day.) She was a pleasant young woman who smoked rather a lot and became shrill with her two small sons when they became unruly, but to her guests she had a very civil tongue, and as New Zealanders inevitably do, we had discovered at least two people whom we knew in common.

Still, it was clear to my quick writer's eyes that she was here for a nefarious purpose, and she certainly did not have the excuse that I did, to exercise my powers of observation. She was hoeing the barbecue in order to watch the couple in the bedroom.

I was very shocked by this. How base is human nature.

She kept on hoeing the barbecue though, and I became nonplussed. She, in her turn, may not understand my legitimate sense of vocation, and might judge me, as I had already judged this interest of hers as prurience.

As I stood there hesitating, my problem was, for the moment, resolved. From behind me a man appeared and approached the motel-keeper's wife. At first I did not recognise him, but then I saw that it was the man in the party of driftwood gatherers. I do not know why he had come to see the motel-keeper's wife but it seemed that he had some transaction to make. I felt rather mortified. It might well have been that she had been waiting for the man to call on her, and that there was nothing sinister about her presence by the barbecue pit after all. Though why, I wondered, was she waiting for the driftwood gatherer out of the sight of her husband? I was beginning to sense corruption and vice all around me.

The driftwood gatherer was a sandy-complexioned man with wispy hair straggling over his collar. I wondered where the woman and child had gone. Away from them, the man looked less remote and romantic, a very ordinary sort of fellow in fact. He and the motel-keeper's wife were standing together now, and she appeared to have given him some money. It was all quite above board, I conceded. He probably did odd jobs for her. She leaned on the handle of her hoe, and he leaned down over the edge of the barbecue, resting his arms on its concrete surrounds. They grinned at each other, and turned their attention towards the room. Neither of them took any notice of me, or seemed to find it strange that I had positioned myself against the fence, casually glancing around as I was, and gazing out to sea now and then.

It was in one of these backwards sweeps that I noted the advance of the Raj woman. Of course, she too had to traverse the path in order to return to her unit.

I became anxious again. Clearly it was most important that

she should be spared any improper sights. I wondered if I should walk along beside her, befriending her, and with my presence, and of course my friendliness, shielding her from the sight of the naked couple on the bed.

She had acquired a long stick which she was using like a staff. She came on up the path towards me. I could not see her eyes behind the dark glasses. But when she was close to me she stopped. The ground was thick with powdery seed heads which seemed to be lying in wait for children to gather them and blow them away. The Raj woman stood still and very deliberately began to knock their heads and appeared to watch the feathering parachutes floating in the evening air. But I saw that her head turned to the window of the room.

Now the sun was flaming yellow gold and about level with where we stood. In the few moments that I had been standing by the Raj woman I had become lonely and ashamed. I had no business to be standing here. If I were to move, surely everyone else would too.

But this now seemed as churlish and high-handed a thing to do, as my previous behaviour had seemed voyeuristic. This is how I put it now, at any rate, for in a story like this, the central character (is that what I was? maybe not, but I am the central core of definition) must be seen to have some finer feelings; I cannot allow you to see her as totally unscrupulous.

The Raj woman had turned her attention to a collection of puffballs now, and was methodically breaking them open with her stick. Some of them were dried up inside and other fresher ones were full of vile squelchy pulp.

There was movement on the bed. The woman was getting up.

For a moment she turned to us, and it seemed that she must surely see us. We saw her smile to herself, that big full-lipped mouth parted over the white teeth. Perhaps she did not see any of us. Maybe she was so full of lust that she was blinded to all outside. Or maybe the gold sun was in her eyes as it set, blinding her.

Whatever it was, I can tell you, that she stood there facing us for a moment so that we saw her quite exquisite breasts and her tapering waist above the brown bush between her legs, and I for one was moved and touched by her beauty. Since the advent of the spa pool I have become much better acquainted with the sight of other women's bodies and I am often moved thus, that quite ordinary women with plain faces can have such magnificent breasts. I have become something of a connoisseur, and there are several women with whom I would gladly change my own rather slight appendages for their springy marble orbs and tender pink nipples. Such a woman was this.

She turned back to the bed, and the man rolled over on his back, welcoming her above him, his hands guiding her in the small of her back.

She had a small tattoo on her right shoulder-blade, carefully positioned as if someone had told her that the eye is drawn to the far side of the right-hand page when it reads, and that we must not be allowed to miss it. The tattoo was of a rose, and it was very pretty.

This was all most disturbing and even more so for the fact that that very afternoon I had been trying to write what I think film makers must generally acknowledge nowadays as the obligatory on-top fuck. I'd wrestled with the images for hours — Bergman's *Fanny and Alexander* (broken wood crying out to broken wood as the bed collapsed), *A Question of Silence* (the Dutch do it too), *Coming Home* (so do war veterans), *Dance With a Stranger* (some women have been hung for less), *The Ploughman's Lunch* (blue skin and middle age in the midnight hours); oh it read like prizegiving night at the Oscars, who did it best? Yes, who, I asked myself.

And here it was, the tattooed lady giving a splendid perform-ance all of her own, with fluttering shoulder-blades and her fingers making a tiny tepee on the coverlet behind her so that she had perfect balance and control, her head thrown back ever so slightly, this was all for her. We could imagine the curve of her throat.

I say we, for beside me the Raj woman's stick was poking at the puffballs and she said to me, 'Nice, very nice isn't it? Isn't it nice?' but she wasn't looking at the ground, and on the seat by the barbecue the motel-keeper's wife was sitting on the drift-wood gatherer's knee with her arms wound passionately around his neck. His hand was up her skirt.

Everyone around me was having such a lovely time, while I was wrestling with art. Surrounded by space, still, I was gasping for air as if I were in a hothouse. It is enough I thought, I cannot bear it any more. I could feel my fingers at work on the keyboard.

But at last the young woman was done, and quite suddenly she sank forward over her lover. The sun, too, had slipped below the horizon and the light began to bleach out of the sky. It was then that I was seized by tenderness and compassion for

the young woman, for I saw that despite her splendid perform-
ance, all could not have been easy for her.

Whereas her lover had such a perfect brown eye to present to
the world she, I saw, had a little pocket of piles. And that, I
thought, thinking of the song, was how one's brown eye turned
to blue.

But whatever the anguish I felt for her, she seemed to be
bearing up well, for now that it was really over, she and her
spent lover (for he was much less sprightly in his actions than
she), came to the window and bowed. We all clapped, and the
curtains were drawn.

Then we, who were outside, shrugged, said good night to
each other in a friendly kind of way, and ambled off in various
directions, the motel-keeper's wife, unhanded now, to her motel
office, the driftwood gatherer to the beach, the Raj woman and
myself to our respective units, she no doubt to finish her novel,
and I to eat avocados and the tongues of lambs, as others might
partake of ambrosia and the tongues of sparrows.

No. This is not true.

Our destinations may have been resolved in such a manner,
I do not remember, or I never knew what happened to the
others, only what I did. Neither is it true that the couple came
to the window, or that we applauded.

Let us reconstruct the scene from a certain point. The dark
simply came upon us all. We came to our senses, or there was
no more to see, and so we slunk away without looking at each
other, not admitting our complicity. And when next I looked
out, it was moonlight, and the curtains were drawn.

That is a possible scenario.

There are certain discrepancies in this story if you know
where to look for them. Let me help you. I have, for instance,
told you that the woman was blinded by the sun. I have also told
you that the motel was on a north-eastern beach. You will see
from this that it would not have been possible for her to have
looked into the sun from this direction. This raises various possibilities. The motel is not where I told you it was after all.
Which raises questions about its existence or not. Or, the
woman was not blinded by the light, and knew that we were
there all the time.

Well I have told you in my opposing scenario that they
bowed. So, what I am telling you is, that they might as well. Oh

who is to know? You will have to decide these things for yourself. You may think I made it all up. Or you may wish to view this as a moral tale. Is it, for instance, immoral to view that which it is intended for us to see (always assuming that the young woman was not blinded by the light), if what we see is a source of delight and pleasure to all, including the participants, or is this in fact, god-like, an excuse to invent new standards for our own viewing pleasure?

You see, as a fledgling film writer, I am having great difficulty with this.

Or, why write this at all? Already I can hear the critics saying, look at Ellen Scumbucket: she takes five thousand words to describe herself watching someone else away at it, and then makes excuses.

Well, what would they have done?

Is that not the question, deep within each and every one of us?

What I do know, and this is absolutely true, is that when the couple left the motel the following morning in their Cordia Turbo, they were both beautifully dressed and turned out, and they both carried briefcases. The young woman's hair was in place and her full mouth was covered afresh with glossy lipstick. She ran her pointed little tongue around the outside edge of her lips and her smile was as sleek and shiny as pudding. Now I think of it, she may have had a little too much.